LOVE LESSONS FOR A LADY

SECRETS OF SCANDALOUS LADIES

BOOK THREE

COLLETTE CAMERON®

Copyright © 2021 Blue Rose Romance® LLC
LOVE LESSONS FOR A LADY
Secrets of Scandalous Ladies
Book 3

Cover Art: Shannon Gilmore

All Rights Reserved

For permission requests, write to the publisher at the address below.
Attn: Permissions Coordinator
info@collettecameronbooks.com
collettecameronbooks.com
eBook ISBN: 978-1-955259-97-2
Print Book ISBN: 978-1-966087-31-1

FREE BOOK!

JOIN MY EXCLUSIVE MAILING LIST
Collette Cameron Newsletter

AND GET A FREE EBOOK!

https://collettecameronbooks.com/freegift

Plus Sneak Peeks, Giveaways, Contests, Exclusive Content, and More... P.S. I promise only good stuff ~ **no** spam!

★★★★★ "The characters were well-crafted, the MCs lovable and worth investigating time in. The plot was clean, and the inspirational bits weren't preachy. I'd happily read more books by Collette Cameron if this is a good example of what I can expect from her." ~ *M. Kittles*

DEDICATION

For the Cheris who helped name the saucy maid, Josie, and the
Mama kitty, and her three kittens.
Thank you, Dee Foster, Catherine Crocker, Fiona Murphy,
Barbara Rogers,
and Jessica Downing.

ACKNOWLEDGMENTS

Thank you to Janet Barret for her clever way of explaining the spelling of Chasity's name.
Thanks also to my talented cover artist Jaycee Lorenzo and to my amazing editor Christy Caughie.

ONE

It's far past time you took your birthright and social position seriously, Aston. I've had enough of my grandson galivanting about the country like a lowborn gypsy. You humiliate and degrade yourself and our family's noble name with your obstinate, uncouth behavior. Your latest escapade is beyond the pale. I demand you cease teaching dance and music lessons at that finishing school and call upon me at Sutton House within the week. I have an important matter to put to you. Defy me in this, Aston, and I promise you the consequences will be dire and far-reaching.

~ Milton Terramier, Viscount Woolbury,
in another threatening letter
to his grandson, Aston Terramier

London, England
Upper Clapton Street

Mrs. Longsdon's Lodging House
10 August 1818 - morning

A nascent sneer skewed Aston Terramier's mouth upward on one side. Taking a bite of perfectly browned toast smeared with pear preserves, he skimmed the slashing penmanship again.

Galivanting...humiliate...degrade...escapade...beyond the pale...

Dire *and* far-reaching.

Dear Grandpapa is truly frothing.

It might be worth answering his summons just to see the inflexible curmudgeon turn lobster-faced. Sputtering and steaming like a forgotten kettle on a hot stove, the old codger would point his knobby finger at Aston as he had since Aston's parents died when he was three.

In his booming voice, his grandsire would call down the Almighty's wrath—God wisely ignored the insufferable, blasphemous tosspot—and grandfather would launch into a well-rehearsed and impossibly lengthy monologue of Aston's faults and shortcomings. All of which he'd heard so many times, he could recite them by rote in his sleep should he desire to.

He did not.

Nor would Aston respond to the viscount's letter. He'd ignore this directive just as he had the dozens of others delivered over the past eight years. Some missives had been curt two-sentence invectives and others pages and pages of acrid diatribe. Each had been burned to cinders and eventually tossed in the rubbish bin.

It wasn't that Aston couldn't forgive.

He could and had chosen to forgive for *his* benefit, not to absolve his grandfather. Unforgiveness led to bitterness, and Aston was determined not to permit his grandfather any influence over his life. Nevertheless, forgiving and forgetting were two vastly different things. Furthermore, once again subjecting himself to his tyrannical grandfather's demands and expectations was unthinkable.

Toast in hand and his head cocked, Aston paused momentarily in chewing the savory morsel. His gaze fell on his humble yet comfortable accommodations. He could afford better now, but these lodgings had become his home, such as they were.

Mismatched end tables flanked a saggy sofa of an undeterminable shade of reddish-brown beneath the paned window. A dented pewter lamp by which Aston read in the evenings dominated one end table along with three neatly stacked books. As he became quickly bored, he never read one book at a time. A haphazard pile of news sheets, music, and journals topped the other end table.

An oval braided rag rug, faded by time and usage, was centered before the sofa. An overstuffed armchair, even saggier than the sofa and covered with the same peculiar shade of upholstery, sat kitty-corner to the couch and the fire grate.

The only other furnishings in the room were an overflowing bookshelf, a violin in its case, and the scarred table and rickety chair where Aston currently sat. Another chair situated across the table held more books and music sheets.

Situated on the other side of the sagging open door on the far side of the sitting room lay his stark bedchamber containing only a narrow, lumpy bed, a lopsided bureau with a cracked beveled mirror by which to shave, a washstand, and a wardrobe. Two small four-paned windows allowed the morning sun in to warm the drafty room.

He shrugged. The simplicity suited him.

Had it *really* been eight years since he'd stormed from his grandfather's opulent mansion with nothing more than the clothes on his back, vowing never to return?

Aye, it had—since Aston's twentieth birthday.

He'd kept that oath, uttered by a rash, wounded, and enraged young man. Even after all of this time, a surge of molten fury tunneled through his veins at the unwanted memory. By God, he'd never agree to an arranged marriage—to a woman his grandfather picked to boot.

Stop.

Aston deliberately turned his mind from that fateful day. Dredging up unpleasant recollections served no useful purpose. Not, in point of fact, that he looked forward to today's activities with much more enthusiasm.

It was Monday, which meant he was expected at Balderbrook's Institution for Genteel Ladies to teach dance lessons from ten until noon. He did the same on Wednesdays. On Thursdays, he gave violin lessons in the morning and pianoforte lessons in the afternoon at the academy, which required him to stay for luncheon.

He'd become convinced over the weeks that his taking the midday meal at Balderbrook's Institution for Genteel Ladies was not entirely due to convenience as Mrs. Crenshaw, the headmistress, had initially alluded.

Nevertheless, the position paid remarkably well—far above the usual wages for dance and music lessons, in truth. Aston had even acquired several more pupils for private lessons as a result. What was more, he'd signed a contract for an entire year, renewable at his discretion. He'd have been a fool to turn down such a lucrative and secure offer, and Aston was no fool.

However, the finishing school's students—many of the instructors too—gawped at him as if he were a sweetmeat or a pastry they longed to gobble up. He, therefore, kept his demeanor coolly professional, although his wicked sense of humor threatened to burst forth on numerous occasions.

Infatuations were an expected and common hazard of males in his position. Regardless, experience had taught Aston that impressionable young women easily became enamored of male instructors. Even married matrons had been known to develop a *tendre*.

Toward that end, Aston generally selected one of the mousiest instructors to model the dance steps with him, and then he stood to the side and critiqued the students as they paired off and practiced the steps. Truth be told, there was one teacher at Balderbrook's Institution for Genteel Ladies, Miss Chasity Noble, he'd very much like to sweep into his arms and whirl around the dance floor. Unfortunately, she moved with natural feminine grace and was far from dowdy or mousy and, therefore, off-limits.

Willowy with creamy blond hair and dark indigo eyes like the ocean's deepest depths, she barely glanced in his direction these past two months. Miss Noble was all starch and no-nonsense. The quintessence of poise and propriety. When she raised an imperial winged eyebrow at a mischievous or overly enthusiastic student, the girl's remorse was instant and genuine.

In Aston's opinion, the perfectly proper Miss Noble could use a lesson or two *or ten* in having fun and enjoying life. She was far too austere for one so young. But then again, most teachers' employment depended on their severity and self-control.

Shoving the last piece of toast into his mouth, Aston rose from the table that also served as his desk. As he wiped the crumbs from his lips with one hand, he crumpled the letter from his grandfather in the other. A cocky grin tipping his lips upward, he tossed the wad over his shoulder toward the fireplace.

"Huzzah!" he whooped when his mark hit home.

Greedy orange, crimson, and blue flames licked the foolscap before devouring the paper with a series of crackles and snaps in mere seconds. No remorse or regret flooded Aston—only relief.

A cold, wet snout nuzzled Aston's hand, and Roi snuffled into his palm.

He brought his gaze around to his ratty, mongrel dog, whose favorite sleeping spot was the equally ratty armchair. Aston had rescued the pup from the streets two years ago. He'd given the skinny, filthy mutt a regal name—Roi was French for King—simply because it amused him to do so.

He and Roi had become the best of friends and were rarely apart. Roi even accompanied him to his lessons, though the dog snoozed in the dated buggy Aston drove. He and Roi were two lonely wretches making their way in a world that didn't favor outcasts.

Though Aston had been born into the lap of luxury and never wanted for anything—except love, that is—he'd eschewed those comforts for freedom and independence.

Not to mention self-respect and dignity.

He thought he rather understood those unruly, uncouth Americans in that regard. They'd chosen hardship, privation, and adversity rather than succumb to the dictates of what they considered an oppressive ruler.

Never mind that that viewpoint wasn't shared by their British counterparts.

Ideals and experiences skewed one's perspective. Didn't opponents on the battlefield both appeal to the same Almighty God for favor and victory?

"Here you go." Aston offered Roi a piece of toast. "We must be on our way shortly, my friend."

Roi cocked his shaggy ebony head, and though he licked

his chops, he didn't accept the offering. His coal-black-eyed gaze darted to the table.

Once. Twice. Thrice

"Greedy bugger."

Chuckling, Aston forked the remaining small beef steak onto the plate. He added an egg and the disdained piece of buttered toast.

"That was to have been my luncheon, rascal."

He'd have to settle for an apple and another piece of toast. Perhaps, Mrs. Crenshaw would ask him to share the midday meal after dance lessons at Balderbrook's Institution for Genteel Ladies again. She'd done so multiple times this past month, and he'd gratefully accepted. For a finishing school, the menu was surprisingly sumptuous and diverse.

Except...last week, Mrs. Crenshaw had placed her hand upon his knee under the table and given a decidedly unvir-tuous squeeze. Her matronly eyes possessed a hungry, besotted glint for all of her stern and decorous demeanor.

Aston hadn't quite worked out how to discourage her without causing offense. Was Mrs. Crenshaw the sort who became spiteful and vindictive if her overtures were rebuffed?

Weren't all women?

No, upon reflection, forgoing luncheon today at Balderbrook's Institution for Genteel Ladies was a far wiser choice. He'd simply save his appetite for dinner and work out a way to avoid dining at the private seminary henceforth. Except for Thursdays, of course when he was there all day and was expected to eat with the staff. Unless he claimed Roi needed a walk during luncheon and brought his lunch with him as he did the other two days a week.

It was something to seriously consider.

Thank goodness Aston's landlady, Mrs. Longsdon, was an

excellent cook and a generous hostess. As a woman of some girth herself, who possessed a healthy appetite, she provided plentiful meals for her lodgers. If it hadn't been for her taking him in eight years ago and waiving his rents until he earned the monies to pay her, Aston might've starved or ended up on the streets.

Or worse.

Her three sons had died in the Napoleonic Wars, and she needed someone to mother. Aston's parents had drowned in a boating accident when he was three. And yet, he'd resolutely refused to return to his tyrannical grandfather's home after their ugly argument.

Uncle Conley and Aston's cousin Werner, who also lived with Grandfather, were little more than whimpering poltroons. Uncle was usually deep in his cups by late afternoon, and Werner was a sycophant and simpering weakling. If Grandfather's ire was directed toward Aston, then Werner was safe from his wrath. Even if the corny-faced milksop was the rotter who generally caused the mischief Aston was blamed for.

Werner and Uncle Conley had been no more able to stand up to the viscount's autocratic expectations and demands than the letter Aston had just thrown into the fire was capable of remaining uncharred. The viscountcy was doomed with those two next in line to inherit.

After placing the plate of food onto the floor, which Roi tore into with admirable gusto, Aston shrugged into his pecan-brown coat before wrapping his midday meal in a serviette. He tucked the simple fare in the outer pocket of his worn leather satchel. He'd placed today's sheet music for dancing in the larger compartment earlier this morning.

He planned on introducing the students to the waltz today and cringed inwardly upon considering their immature reactions. Alas, no reputable dance instructor eschewed the waltz these days, even if it weren't exactly *de rigueur* in the poshest homes yet.

Roi finished his meal and proceeded to groom himself in a most indecorous fashion.

"Must you behave so unseemly?" Aston raised a mocking eyebrow. "And after dining too?"

Roi snuffled an answer as he continued his morning ablutions.

Aston gathered the dirty dishes and cutlery and placed them on a tray. As was his usual routine, he'd set them outside his door when he left for the day, and they'd be gone when he returned. Mrs. Longsdon preferred that he eat in the dining room with the rest of her boarders, but as a frightened pup, Roi had barked and whined to such an extent that she'd relented and permitted Aston to take his meals in his rooms.

It had become a habit now. Aston paid extra each month for having the dog and for her cleaning his rooms too. She needed the coin, and Aston needed Roi.

After slipping his satchel's strap over one shoulder, Aston placed his top hat on his head. With a snap of his fingers to Roi, he lifted the tray and left his chamber.

Eight years, he mused as he tramped down the corridor, his bag bumping his hip.

Roi's nails clicked a soft staccato on the worn but clean wood floor as he followed at Aston's heels. Extraordinarily intelligent, the dog had trained himself to pace Aston. House training had taken but a week, and the dog could open the door and fetch the news sheets too.

No longer destitute but certainly far from the lofty heights he'd once known, Aston considered his future as he descended the squeaky stairs. He'd become quite sought after in upper circles and had a tidy amount saved in the bank. He suspected much of his elite clientele resulted from his being the grandson of a lord and not Aston's teaching abilities.

Not that he wasn't a dashed good dance master and music teacher because he was. The chasm between Aston and his grandfather was no secret among the *ton*, however. Society liked nothing better than a bit of scintillating controversy as long as an outright scandal wasn't the cause.

The truth of it was, Aston had grown rather bored giving lessons. Restlessness and discontent had leeched into his simple, orderly life. He wanted something else. Something more. Something undefinable he couldn't quite put his finger on.

Miss Chasity Noble's delicate features flashed across his mind, and a slow smile arced Aston's mouth upward. Why yes. A flirtation with the prim beauty might be just the sort of pleasant distraction he needed.

As long as Mrs. Crenshaw didn't grow wise to his intent.

TWO

Yes, I have wondered who went to the effort to see us secretly placed at Haven House and Academy for the Enrichment of Young Women. I shall also confess to a natural curiosity about my parentage. But, in truth, I don't want to know who placed me in the home or why. It would change nothing. I believe we are better off accepting our circumstances and pointing our energy and focus forward, not backward.

~ Miss Chasity Noble in response
to a letter from Miss Mercy Feathers,
now Mercy Brockman

London Outskirts
Balderbrook's Institution for Genteel Ladies
10 August 1818 - midmorning

Why on earth did Chasity recall that letter now of all times?

It had been over five years since she'd answered Mercy's question. Unlike many of her friends, including Mercy, also raised at Haven House and Academy for the Enrichment of

Young Women, Chasity didn't possess a driving need to know why she'd been abandoned or who her parents were.

Honestly, she didn't even mind that a careless, near-sighted cleric had recorded her name as Chasity Thomasina Lilith Shepard Noble, missing the other 't' in Chastity.

Skimming her gaze over two dozen bent heads, she curved her mouth into a half-smile at the tableau before her. Four-and-twenty girls ranging in age from twelve to seventeen met her perusal within the four tidy rows of desks. This was her life, or at least it had been for the past two months and would be until she retired several decades from now.

A pang of regret twinged near the region of her heart, but she stoically dismissed the nostalgia. So her destiny didn't include marriage and children. There were many, many worse things. Chasity was one of the lucky ones. *She* held a reliable position and needn't fret about her future.

At five-and-twenty, Chasity had become assistant head-mistress at one of Balderbrook's Institution for Genteel Ladies private seminaries. Before that, she'd been the etiquette, French, and writing instructor at another branch of Balderbrook's Institution for Genteel Ladies. When she'd been asked to consider the promotion to assistant head-mistress at the school's new location, she'd leaped at the opportunity.

What woman in her position wouldn't have?

Lady Jane Balderbrook—the seminary's namesake and chief patron—had put forth the suggestion to Chasity's former headmistress.

Rarely did one so young get offered such a prestigious position. Chasity could only credit her diligence and dedication in performing her duties in her previous post, and Lady Balderbrook's personal recommendation, of course, for the advancement.

And my total lack of interest in finding a beau and marrying.

Marriage was not Chasity's ultimate goal, unlike the girls seated before her. She was expected to mold them into the epitome of refinement so they might marry and efficiently manage their own households one day.

As assistant headmistress, she had her own rooms, a larger salary, and most importantly, security. *Security and stability.* Those mattered most to her. Instructors came and went, but headmistresses and their assistants could anticipate a lengthy career if they so chose. And if they minded themselves most diligently.

Glancing at the miniature brass table clock angled on one corner of her practical desk, she cleared her throat.

"Girls, it's nearly time for dance lessons."

A chorus of muted giggles erupted behind hands clasped over mouths. Half of the students were smitten with the dance master. The other half were tongue-tied and awestruck in his presence.

In Chasity's opinion, Aston Terramier was too young and attractive to be a suitable dance master or music teacher. His form and features proved most distracting to the impression-able students. They were forever *forgetting* their steps and asking him to personally instruct them.

A hunch-backed, arthritic, doddering soul nearing his eighth decade and hard of hearing would serve quite well instead. Just such a gentleman had taught the proper dance steps to the students at Haven House and Academy for the Enrichment of Young Women.

To his credit, Mr. Terramier skillfully deflected the girls' attempts for private lessons and demonstrated the movements with one of the teachers. Usually, Pomposa Wetherwax, Stella Ramsbottom, or Geraldine Belcher. All of whom were long in the tooth, longer on the shelf, portly, and as awkward on the dance floor as blindfolded hippopotamuses in high heels.

"Ahem."

Chasity cleared her throat again, and at once, the school-room settled into an energetic quiet. The students fairly vibrated with anticipation. She supposed she couldn't blame them. Mrs. Crenshaw didn't employ any footmen for obvious reasons. It wouldn't do to have young men in such close proximity to so many impressionable girls.

The only males present at the school were two middling-aged grooms, who also acted as coachmen and stable hands, and an aged, arthritic gardener.

The men who delivered the firewood, milk, and various other supplies from time to time were rarely seen by residents at Balderbrook's Institution for Genteel Ladies except for Mrs. Pottkotter—the cook—or the four maids. Or Chasity, who typically rose at five for a constitutional before her lengthy day as assistant headmistress began.

"Return your books to your chambers, collect your gloves, and then make your way to the ballroom in an orderly fashion." Chasity stood and shook out her navy-blue muslin gown before patting her tidy chignon. Removing her plain white gloves from a desk drawer, she said, "Remember to keep your backs straight and walk with the grace and decorum you've been practicing."

A stickler for convention, Mrs. Crenshaw threatened to make any girl with less than perfect posture wear a backboard. Those devices were unnatural and cruel, and thus far, Chasity had been able to dissuade the headmistress from actually carrying out her threat.

"I shouldn't think Mr. Terramier expects to instruct hoydens today," she said as she slipped her gloves on.

"Yes, Miss Noble," came the expected subdued chorus.

Nonetheless, undisguised eagerness shimmered in the girls' eyes.

Chasity suppressed a sigh and resisted rolling her eyes ceilingward.

They'd take hours to settle down this afternoon. Perhaps a nature walk and foliage sketching were in order. *If* she could convince the headmistress and other instructors. A glance at the windows lining the room's far side confirmed the weather was pleasant enough. In truth, the afternoon might prove too warm to venture outdoors.

The students filed from the schoolroom, but once they made the corridor, more giggles erupted. There was also the unmistakable echo of running footsteps and loud whispering.

Harnessing a swarm of bees was easier than subduing healthy, spirited girls. It always pained Chasity to stifle their natural liveliness and exuberance, but her duty was to mold them into young ladies—not indulge or encourage madcap behavior.

Perhaps she would excuse herself from overseeing the dance lessons today. Six other instructors were surely sufficient for the forty-and-seven girls. The seminary boasted beds for seventy students, but the facility wasn't yet fully staffed and adding additional students wasn't prudent.

Besides, she hadn't yet updated the financial records. Mrs. Crenshaw was competent and organized, but Chasity's mathematical abilities surpassed the headmistress's. Once Rafaela Crenshaw had learned of Chasity's skill with numbers, she'd gladly transferred the bookkeeping obligations.

With a final glance around her classroom, Chasity made a mental note to water the fern in the corner this afternoon. The plant was her only concession to personalizing the room. As she made her way along the well-scrubbed and stark dark-paneled, rather gloomy corridor to the headmistress's office, she mulled over the two open positions at this branch of Balderbrook's Institution for Genteel Young Ladies.

If only one or more of her friends from Haven House and Academy for the Enrichment of Young Women could be persuaded to apply for them. Faith, Purity, Trinity, or Honoria would be a good fit. She was sure of it. Chasity selfishly wanted one of her girlhood friends here. Though she got on well with the instructors and headmistress, she didn't quite fit in with the older, stuffier women either.

In truth, she was lonely.

I'll write to them again tonight. These positions are certain to be filled soon.

There had been dozens and dozens of applicants, but Mrs. Crenshaw was nothing if not persnickety and meticulous. More than once, Chasity wondered if she'd have been selected as assistant headmistress had it been Mrs. Crenshaw's decision to make.

It hadn't been, and Chasity felt more relief about that fact than was warranted. Mrs. Crenshaw had never said anything or implied disapproval in any way. Nevertheless, Chasity had seen her observing her with slightly narrowed, watery teabrown eyes and a pinched expression about her thin mouth and pointed nose more than once.

Finishing school instructors weren't supposed to be young and attractive. Even if they were rather a whiz with numbers and calculations. And languages too. Chasity was fluent in four and could speak another three. Alas, there wasn't much use for Latin or Greek in a girls' seminary.

Even Mrs. Crenshaw believed she only spoke French, Italian, and German. Chasity thought it best not to show up the other instructors or the headmistress, all of whom spoke fluent French but naught else to her knowledge.

Toward that end, Chasity did everything within her power

to appear plain and inconspicuous. Her clothing was staid and practical, as was her neat chignon. She never wore jewelry except for the silver cross gifted to her by Hester Shepherd, the proprietress of Haven House and Academy for the Enrichment of Young Women when Chasity left the home for her first position. The cross was only worn for special occasions at that, and it was by no means flamboyant or gaudy.

Giving her head a slight shake to dispel her unnerving musings, she rapped once upon Mrs. Crenshaw's office door.

Silence met her query. Unusual, that.

Chasity canted her head, listening.

After pausing for several heartbeats, she knocked again.

"Mrs. Crenshaw?"

"Come in," came the headmistress's muffled summons.

Chasity entered and paused just inside the entrance, waiting the bid to advance further.

Spectacles low on her nose and forehead furrowed, Mrs. Crenshaw stared at the foolscap before her on the immaculate desk. As Chasity observed her, the woman's mouth went taut, as did her shoulders. Something very near a scowl creased the headmistress's face.

At last, she glanced upward, her countenance once more returned to inscrutable.

Before Chasity could ask to be excused from supervising, Mrs. Crenshaw said, "You'll have to manage the dance instructions today, Miss Noble. I have an urgent correspondence that I must respond to posthaste."

Mrs. Crenshaw rustled the paper atop her glossy desk between her forefinger and thumb.

So much for finishing the accounts this morning. The task would have to be postponed until after supper. Chasity gave a mental shrug. The book she was reading, *The Influence of Literature Upon Society*, wasn't riveting, and she could definitely wait to get back to it. In truth, she was only reading the tome because it helped calm her mind so she could drift off to sleep.

She eyed the miffed headmistress from beneath her eyelashes.

This temperamental display was most unusual. Most rare indeed. Mrs. Crenshaw's ability to mask her emotions was rather eerie. That she revealed even an iota of what she felt stirred Chasity's curiosity.

How could it not?

The rapid rise and fall of Mrs. Crenshaw's scarecrowish chest, the reflexive tightening of her bony hand upon the edge of the desk, and the repetitive thinning of her lips into a taut line revealed the usually unflappable woman's distress.

Chasity's attention gravitated to the letter. The wax seal wasn't visible, but bold penmanship lashed the page.

Peering at the missive, Mrs. Crenshaw made a slight noise in her throat that might've been exasperation or aggravation.

Whatever could've upset her to such an extent she must forego dance lessons and pen a prompt response? The headmistress hadn't missed a dance lesson since the school opened. In point of fact, Chasity suspected Mrs. Crenshaw might be mildly infatuated with the engaging and much younger Mr. Terramier.

With a start, Chasity realized she hadn't responded to Mrs. Crenshaw's directive to oversee the dance lessons this morning. "Of course, Mrs. Crenshaw. I would be happy to supervise."

Perhaps not happy, but assuredly capable.

Before Chasity reached the doorway, the headmistress had pulled a piece of foolscap from the desk drawer and dipped the quill into the inkpot.

"Miss Noble?"

Chasity glanced behind her and half-turned. "Yes?"

Mrs. Crenshaw paused, her quill in mid-air.

"Do invite Mr. Terramier to stay for luncheon. I had Cook prepare stuffed partridge and herbed potatoes and carrots. Also, a lemon tart. A particular favorite of his." *How does she know that?* "I should be finished with this task by then."

And why does Mr. Terramier garner stuffed partridge when cold meats, cheese, fruit, and bread sufficed for luncheon for the girls and staff most days? If Chasity had any lingering doubts that Mrs. Crenshaw meant to impress the dance instructor, they promptly dissolved.

"I'm certain you and the other teachers can entertain Mr. Terramier on my behalf," Mrs. Crenshaw said, returning her focus to the paper before her and obviously not expecting a response.

On *her* behalf, was it?

His wasn't a social call, for pity's sake.

A prickle of unease marched along Chasity's spine as she nodded, turned, and exited. Quietly closing the door behind her, she bit her lower lip, unable to dispel the sense of disquiet that had crept over her like early morning dew on a field.

Was it due to the unknown contents of the letter or Mrs. Crenshaw's inappropriate *tendre* for Mr. Terramier? Or was the disquieting undercurrent something else entirely?

THREE

Do say you can come for tea the Sunday after next. It will be a relatively small gathering, according to my new mother-in-law. Although her idea of small and mine are somewhat different. I've missed you so, Chasity, and we are off to Kelvingrove Park next week for an extended house party. I know you only have two half-days off each month, but I can send a carriage 'round for you. Faith will be there, and Joy and her husband are in London visiting too. Please, dearest, do say you'll come.

~ Mercy Brockman in an invitation
to tea for Miss Chasity Noble

Balderbrook's Institution for Genteel Ladies
Outside the ballroom

Girlish laughter reigned in Chasity's maudlin musings. *Ah, yes.* The dance lessons, and by the sound of the copious giggling and *sotto voce* whispering, Mr. Terramier had indeed arrived.

Josie, one of the maids, hurried down the corridor, a stack

of neatly folded clean table linens in her arms. She grinned at Chasity and rolled her eyes toward the ballroom. "His gorgeousness is here."

She really ought to be reprimanded for her impertinence, but Chasity found Josie's bluntness rather refreshing.

"Please tell Mrs. Pottkotter that I've been instructed to ask Mr. Terramier to stay for luncheon." Chasity wanted to ensure that no one drew the wrong conclusion and thought the invitation was her idea.

"Of course, his handsomeness has." Josie giggled and, after scanning the corridor, edged nearer to Chasity. She waggled her eyebrows mischievously. "Mrs. Crenshaw is after him like a she-cat in heat."

Josie was nothing if not blunt.

Chasity nearly choked on a stifled laugh. "That will be all, Josie."

"Yes, Miss Noble." As if she'd realized she'd crossed the mark, Josie ducked her chin to her chest and bobbed a curtsy. "I beg your pardon."

She hurried on her way, but Chasity had the distinct impression the impudent minx didn't harbor any genuine remorse. Josie had best be careful because neither the other instructors nor Mrs. Crenshaw would be as forgiving.

In short order, Chasity gained the ballroom and swiftly took in the situation. Pomposa Wetherwax sat before the rosewood pianoforte on a tufted red velvet bench. An unbecoming shade of red blotched her rounded cheeks as Mr. Terramier arranged whatever music he had selected for today's lessons before her.

His words floated to Chasity as she approached.

"Are you familiar with the music, Mrs. Wetherwax?"

Only Chasity went by *Miss* even though none of the instructors had ever been married. Mrs. was deemed more respectable, but perhaps because of her youth, or possibly to make a point Chasity had yet to decipher, she alone was permitted to be addressed as Miss rather than Mrs.

"Indeed, Mr. Terramier," Mrs. Wetherwax simpered, coyly batting her stubby eyelashes.

She looked utterly ridiculous, and pity for the smitten woman pricked Chasity.

"I am *most* familiar and only too happy to *accommodate* you," Mrs. Weatherwax gushed.

A double entendre if Chasity had ever heard one.

Mr. Terramier glanced upward as Chasity crossed the room, silently ordering the girls to settle down with a stern glance and a raised brow. Their tittering diminished in volume but didn't entirely go away.

And why should it?

They were young girls, after all, and dancing was a favorite pastime. Did they not deserve a bit of joy in their young lives? Why must children be compelled to behave like miniature grownups? Adulthood wasn't so very wonderful with all of its expectations, rules, and disappointments.

A beam of sunlight from the small row of leaded glass windows high along the far side of the room illuminated Mr. Terramier's sculpted face. Despite her avowal to remain unaffected, Chasity's pulse quickened.

Gracious me. Those eyes.

That nose. Those cheeks. That chin.

All looked to have been carved by a master sculptor.

But then, wasn't that precisely what the Good Lord was? A master sculptor?

Mr. Terramier's dark, slightly wavy hair glistened as if styled with the finest almond oil. He possessed shoulders too broad, a chest too wide, and legs too long to be considered fashionable among the *ton*.

What did *le beau monde* know of masculine perfection anyway with its preference for overly slim, pale-faced lords or those who boasted paunchy stomachs and swollen faces from overindulgence?

With the aura of light as a backdrop to his masculine beauty, Mr. Terramier appeared otherworldly. Almost godlike. Such imaginations from a woman raised by the poised and deeply religious Hester Shepherd bordered on blasphemous.

Chasity gave the tiniest disdainful sniff.

Godlike indeed.

She blamed her ridiculous comparison to momentary light-headedness. She'd skipped breakfast and hadn't eaten heartily of last night's dinner—mutton stew. She didn't favor mutton. Unfortunately, as mutton was less expensive than beef, it was often on the menu.

Which begged the question, why were they eating partridge for luncheon today? Undoubtedly, such luxuries strained the school's budget, particularly as they weren't yet at capacity and hadn't the extra tuition to offset expenses.

"Good day, Miss Noble."

Mr. Terramier bent into a bow a courtier would've been proud of. The courtesy was unnecessary and caused a collective sigh to go up in the room, followed by another round of muffled sniggering from the students.

And a shrewd narrowing of eyes from a few of the envious instructors.

Botheration.

That wouldn't do at all.

Though Chasity was the assistant headmistress, the other women outnumbered her. All it would take is the merest hint of scandal, and she'd be out the door without a reference. A tarnished reputation was the downfall of many a governess or instructor, whether there was any merit behind their smudged character or not.

Which was why Chasity guarded the secret of her paternity with such care—or rather her illegitimacy. Only Mrs. Hester Shepherd, the proprietress of Haven House and Academy for the Enrichment of Young Women, and whoever had placed the girls at the foundling home knew the cast-offs' parentage.

An intrepid, pious woman, Mrs. Shepherd named every girl under her care and tutelage, giving each a version of her own surname. Hence every by-blow who left the institution did so with Shephard as one of their surnames. Mrs. Shepherd, who'd never had children of her own, said all of the girls entrusted to her care were as dear as daughters to her.

And yet, she'd warned her charges to never reveal the disgrace of their paternity.

"It's unjust to be sure, but many are those who would dismiss you, snub you, and disparage your character for the sins of your parents," Mrs. Shepherd had said numerous times. "Should the question come up, you may say your parents have gone on. That is not a lie because they may have died, and they assuredly have gone on with their lives if they are yet amongst the living."

Mrs. Shepherd was as shrewd as she was devout.

"Good day, Mr. Terramier." Chasity kept her tone coolly professional. "Mrs. Crenshaw sends her regrets. She cannot join us for dance lessons today. However, she expects to have finished her task by luncheon and hopes you'll dine with us."

Even to her ears, the invitation sounded flat and insincere. If Mrs. Crenshaw hadn't finished her letter, did she expect Chasity to entertain him?

"I would be delighted." Mr. Terramier flashed her a blinding grin, and Chasity blinked up at him rather stupidly.

Good Lord above.

Now she understood far-sighted Pomposa Wetherwax's befuddlement and her big-as-a-dinner-plate eyes behind her thick spectacles.

Smiles that scattered one's wits, flopped one's tummy over itself, and unhinged one's knees ought to be against the law. A scripture about resisting temptation fluttered around the edges of Chasity's conscience but faded away before she could seize upon it like a drowning kitten.

Regaining her composure, she folded her hands before her. She must model how she expected the students to behave. From beneath her eyelashes, she observed Stella Ramsbottom fervently whispering into Geraldine Belcher's ear.

Practically—no, *actually*—ogling Mr. Terramier, Geraldine nodded vigorously.

They, too, ought to be modeling decorum instead of acting like calf-eyed ninnies in front of the students.

"Shall we begin?" Chasity angled her chin toward the students. "Girls, form your lines, please. Quickly and quietly."

They complied at once, every moon-eyed student's attention fixated on Mr. Terramier.

Oh, this really was too much.

Chasity fought the urge to grind her teeth into powder or melodramatically roll her eyes. Really, hadn't any of them a smidge of restraint or a modicum of pride? They all looked like love-sick dolts.

Mrs. Wetherwax ran her thick fingers over the keys, practicing the first few stanzas of the waltz. Chasity wasn't familiar with the melody, but it possessed a lilting quality that made her want to tap her toes.

"I had intended to ask Mrs. Crenshaw to help me demonstrate the dance movements today," Mr. Terramier said in his melodic baritone.

Mrs. Crenshaw would be terribly disappointed.

"As she's not available, you'll have to select one of the instructors in her stead," Chasity said, indicating with an angled shoulder the cluster of enthusiastic teachers.

Each wore a pathetic expression of eager anticipation. Once a wallflower, always a wallflower, it would seem.

"Ah, yes. Although..." Mr. Terramier mused with mock thoughtfulness, the rich timbre of his voice reverberating in his chest as he held a forefinger to his strong chin.

Did the man sing too?

Where had that ridiculous thought come from?

Before Chasity could wrestle her equanimity into submission, he flashed another dashing grin. His thickly lashed, rich brown eyes fairly smoldered with amusement.

Why. Why, the bounder was laughing at Chasity!

He knew exactly how he affected her, the insolent cur. Well, she was not one to be trifled with by the likes of him. She was made of sterner stuff, and no handsome buck would turn her head.

"Mr. Terramier. We await your selection," she prompted with remarkable civility, quite proud she could affect an unflustered demeanor. Never mind the rabbits hopping about in her stomach.

"Oh, but I cannot possibly pick one of them without hurting the others' feelings," Mr. Terramier murmured near her ear as he took her elbow. His voice practically a purr, he said, "Much wiser to select you as a partner, Miss Noble, I think."

What? *What?*

Had he mistaken her meaning, or was he being deliberately obtuse?

Chasity shrewdly eyed him.

He grinned. Unrepentant and unabashed.

The latter. Most definitely the latter, the rotter.

He guided her forward.

"Wh...what are you d...doing?" she asked, cursing inwardly at her tongue-tied stutter.

She did not stammer. Or hadn't until this moment. But when Mr. Terramier wrapped his long fingers around her arm, her tongue thickened to thrice its normal size and seemed incapable of forming words.

"Giving you a lesson." His smile broadened with something akin to primal satisfaction. His impressive back to the others, the scoundrel winked.

The knave actually winked.

Chasity had the distinct impression a dance lesson was not what he referred to, and she fought to keep her face serene and not jerk her arm free. Painfully aware of the many pairs of eyes avidly watching her and Mr. Terramier, she whispered, "I *cannot* dance with you."

"Of course, you can," came his glib, wholly unapologetic reply as he led her to the front of the room. "Who can object to a harmless *lesson*?"

Again, the odd inflection on the word.

The heat of his palm burned through the fabric of her sensible gown, branding her. When she disrobed tonight, she wouldn't be at all surprised to find the outline of a palm print upon her flesh. She cast a hasty glance toward the other teachers and immediately regretted the impulse.

Open hostility or betrayal etched deep lines into their aging faces.

Oh dear.

Prepared to give him a set-down, Chasity turned her face upward to meet his scintillating chocolate-eyed gaze. And promptly forgot what she was about to say.

"You do know how to waltz, do you not, Miss Noble?"

FOUR

No, Werner, I cannot assist you. Unlike you, I actually work for a living, and I shan't waste my hard-earned coin to remedy your feckless, irresponsible conduct. This time you cannot shift the blame to me for your behavior. Your penchant for whoring, racing, and gambling has landed you in your dire predicament. I suggest you appeal to our grandfather for the funds you require to pay your debts. I also advise you in the future to not borrow money from known captain sharks.

~ Aston Terramier in a letter
to his cousin, Werner Terramier
Sent but intercepted by Viscount Woolbury

Balderbrook's Institution for Genteel Ladies' ballroom
Thirty extremely awkward seconds later

"Of course, I *know* how to waltz, Mr. Terramier. However, as assistant headmistress, it is hardly proper for me to do so," Miss Noble hissed beneath her breath. "I must consider appearances."

Her argument held no merit, and they both knew it.

If Mrs. Crenshaw could practice with the dance master, no one could find fault for Miss Noble doing so as well. She fashioned a weak smile and sent it toward the glowering teachers. When their hardened countenances didn't soften a jot, Aston realized his mistake.

Blister and blast.

He'd put Miss Noble in an untenable position. As the only beauty among her peers and the youngest in a position of authority, she'd already roused their envy. Aston's yielding to a selfish urge to hold her in his arms also made her a target of their jealousy.

Flashing his most disarming smile, he took in the other women one by one. He kept his attention on each instructor, waiting until pleased color suffused her cheeks or she bashfully dropped her gaze before he moved to the next. He well knew how to charm a lady into doing his bidding, though he was loath to do so under false pretenses.

Nonetheless, in this case, he had little recourse. He must diffuse the other teachers' antagonism.

"I shall begin today's instructions with the most basic waltz. However, I feel for the students to properly grasp the elegance, precision, and subtle complexities of the waltz's steps, as well as the various types of popular waltzes, I shall need to demonstrate with each instructor who is willing to indulge me today and Wednesday. And, if necessary, next week as well. We shall not move on to the allemande until the students have mastered the waltz to my satisfaction."

That brought little forgiving nods of approval from the

teachers and envious sighs from the older students. If Aston wasn't a dashed good dance master and if he didn't enjoy dancing so much himself, he'd abandon the occupation in a thrice.

Well, and if he didn't need the funds to support himself. Hopefully, the venture he'd recently invested in would prove prosperous, and he could consider putting his career as a dance master behind him.

He'd need to find something else to aggravate his grandfather, however, else the man would have nothing to do with his days. Viscount Woolbury was happiest when in high dudgeon. Only, Aston suspected Werner might be graying what few hairs remained on their grandfather's pate.

Summoning a smile, Aston tilted his head toward the teachers. "Ladies? If you would be so kind."

Momentarily appeased, the other instructors took their places, supervising the two lines of eager students.

He released Chasity's elbow, murmuring beneath his breath for her ears alone, "Will that suffice to salve their wounded sensibilities?"

A slight furrow knitted Chasity's delicate eyebrows together as she took her place, and her blue eyes turned impossibly more tumultuous. Aston could stare into the depths of her expressive eyes indefinitely. He now understood how the mythical Greek sirens entrapped men with little more than a seductive song.

"I honestly don't know." Worry shadowed her arresting eyes and creased the outer corners. "You shouldn't have provoked them like that," Miss Noble chastised, sending her fellow instructors a sidelong glance, and her jaw tightened. "They'll blame me."

She's worried about repercussions.

Simply because Aston had asked her to assist him for the

first time in two months? How many times had he partnered with the others and never witnessed such sullenness?

Were women really so shallow and spiteful?

Even spinsters long on the shelf?

He hadn't much experience with women. There'd been plenty of opportunities for liaisons, and he'd indulged in a few innocent flirtations over the years. The truth was, however, he was rather old-fashioned, and none of those flirtations had ever gone any further.

Miss Noble swept into position across from him. She moved with a natural elegance other women strived for and often never attained. Not even aristocrats who trained for years in finishing schools such as Balderbrook's Institution for Genteel Ladies. Furthermore, Miss Chasity Noble seemed utterly guileless. In his limited experience, a rare thing for a beautiful woman.

"Forgive me, Miss Noble. I meant no harm. I assure you. I vow I didn't mean to place you in a difficult position." Aston hadn't and regretted if he'd caused her difficulty with her fellow instructors.

She tilted her head and presented him with a practiced half-smile. "Naught to do but soldier on now."

He'd bet she used that small upward bend of her mouth when she taught too. Her self-discipline was admirable, but he wanted to see the woman beneath the polished, controlled exterior. The real Chasity Noble.

His gaze dipped to her full, peach-tinted lips.

Had she ever been kissed?

Aston wagered not.

He notched his chin toward Mrs. Wetherwax, who fell to playing with aplomb if not particular skill.

"As we've discussed before," he explained to the gawpeyed students, "each dance begins and ends with a bow or curtsy."

He made a leg toward Chasity, and she dipped into a sophisticated curtsy.

"There are many variations of the waltz," Aston said. "We shall begin with the most basic. The male partner places his right hand like this."

Giggling and rustling filled the room as the girl who'd agreed to play the male did as he instructed.

He rested his palm upon Chasity's trim waist, and a shock of electricity coursed through him. Stiffening, she gasped, a soft whoosh of air passing between her lips. Her sapphire gaze flew to his for an instant before darting away just as speedily.

He'd not been alone in experiencing the jolting sensation then.

This was a terrible idea indeed. Merely being in close proximity with Chasity had Aston aware of her in a way no dance master should be. He swallowed and concentrated on the pupils' annoying twittering. That cooled his unexpected ardor in a trice.

"And the female places her left hand, light as thistledown, upon her partner's shoulder," he said in a voice uncharacteristically thick.

Without meeting Aston's eyes, Chasity rested a palm ever so gently upon his shoulder. Face averted, she allowed him to take her hand. The downy blond hairs along her nape begged him to brush his lips across the ivory flesh just there. To see if it was as smooth as it looked.

A faint scent of lemon and floral soap wafted past his nostrils—heady and intoxicating. Despite their audience, he inhaled Chasity's essence deep into his lungs. Giving himself a vigorous mental shake, Aston focused on the dance steps.

Mrs. Wetherwax continued tormenting the pianoforte by

pounding the keys with the exuberance of a pugilist during a boxing match. The unfortunate instrument was losing the battle. Badly.

Raising his voice, Aston directed the students as he and Chasity demonstrated the various steps. Time stood still and simultaneously raced along as they went through the motions.

She steadfastly kept her gaze riveted on his coat lapels, the tips of her lush lashes feathery and almost translucent. Her alabaster skin was as soft and smooth as a white rose petal. He'd never noticed the texture of a woman's skin before, but somehow, he knew hers wasn't typical.

A discordant chord jangled him out of his reverie, and he drew to a halt. He cleared his voice. "Let's change partners, shall we? Mrs. Ramsbottom, would you do the honors of demonstrating next?"

"I should be delighted," preened the stout woman, smiling widely and revealing the substantial gap between her front teeth.

"Yes, yes," Chasity murmured, slightly winded.

Aston would warrant her shortness of breath wasn't from over-exertion either.

"I shall check on Mrs. Crenshaw and upon our luncheon," she said to the room at large. Her color high, she bobbed Aston a hasty curtsy.

Generally, she was across the table from him when they dined with Mrs. Crenshaw seated at the head between them. He didn't dare displace an instructor by claiming their seat for himself either. Position, even at the dining table, was everything in establishments such as Balderbrook's Institution for Genteel Ladies.

Aston bowed. "Until luncheon, Miss Noble."

As she swept from the ballroom without a backward glance, he recalled his decision this morning not to accept any more midday meal invitations from the headmistress. But how else was he to engage in a flirtation with the lovely Miss Noble if he eschewed such an opportunity?

Even as he justified his reasoning, Aston knew full well he ought not to stay. An open flirtation with Miss Noble was out of the question, particularly as Mrs. Crenshaw had made known her unprofessional awareness of him. He rather suspected the older woman capable of vindictiveness if she discovered his interest lay in the much younger and much more attractive assistant headmistress.

In truth, he ought to resign his position at the seminary before things became more complicated. However, to do so would give his crusty old grandfather a victory. That was something Aston wasn't willing to concede to the curmudgeon. He'd simply have to don a cool, unapproachable façade to discourage untoward romantic notions from the students, instructor, or headmistress.

As he watched Chasity's lithe form disappear through the double doors, he sighed. Regretfully, the flirtation that held such appeal earlier today was not meant to be.

Marshaling a smile, he extended his hand. "Mrs. Ramsbottom. Shall we?"

Why did such disappointment cinch his ribs?

FIVE

As the headmistress, I presume that you are an intelligent woman, well-versed in society's strictures. I am certain you understand my position, Mrs. Crenshaw. Not only is it gauche and vulgar, but it is also far beneath my grandson to act as a dance and music instructor—particularly for payment. It casts an unsavory shadow over the viscountcy and our family's name. It would behoove you to search for another dancing master at your earliest convenience as I do not foresee Aston remaining in your employ. What a shame it would be if Balderbrook's Institution for Genteel Ladies were to have to close its doors. Scandals are such cruel and fickle creatures. I am confident you take my meaning.

~ Viscount Woolbury in a letter
to Mrs. Rafaela Crenshaw

London, England

Balderbrook's Institution for Genteel Ladies
13 August 1818 - morning

Chasity bent over the ledger, adding the row of figures for the fourth time.

Dash it all.

She blamed her distractedness on *him*—Aston Terramier. He'd arrived an hour ago, and her traitorous mind kept replaying those few moments he'd whirled her around the dance floor on Monday.

Truth be told, she'd replayed those minutes many times in the past three days.

Wednesday morning, she'd awoken with a blistering headache and begged off supervising dance lessons. Mrs. Crenshaw had been oddly solicitous and hadn't seemed the least put out when Chasity had missed luncheon as well. A dose of headache powders, a cold cloth across her forehead, and a nap had worked wonders.

Calling Chasity's recovery remarkable, the headmistress had gratefully turned over supervision of the afternoon activities to Chasity and disappeared into her office. A habit increasing in frequency and which had been remarked upon by the other teachers.

They did not appreciate the authority Chasity had been granted, although it was more like foisting off responsibilities to her way of thinking. It was hardly her place to refuse Mrs. Crenshaw, which put her in an untenable position.

To avoid Mr. Terramier today, because Chasity didn't trust herself not to go all giddy again, she'd seized upon her regular Thursday morning routine. She'd sequestered herself inside her office and attended to correspondence, bookkeeping, and any other tasks Mrs. Crenshaw sent her way.

Tasks which also seemed to increase every week.

Naturally, as assistant headmistress, Chasity bore a heavier workload than the other instructors. Regardless, she couldn't help but suspect that Mrs. Crenshaw was taking advantage of Chasity's benevolence and her abilities.

Quill poised between her fingertips, she cocked her head and listened. The deep, dulcet tones of Aston's rich baritone carried to her. A glance out the open window confirmed that the music room doors were spread wide to allow the fragrant, cooling breeze inside.

Outside, industrious bees zipped between a rainbow of summer blossoms. Sunny yellow, violet, fuchsia, and orange dahlias. Red, purple, and pink zinnias. Sweet peas in shades of pink, coral, and lavender. And roses, of course, although the bees didn't generally pay much attention to those blooms.

Chasity flinched, splattering ink droplets atop the journal as his second pupil of the morn, Esmerelda Finch-Hatten, tortured the violin's strings.

God save me.

Chasity loathed music lessons worse than dance instructions. Half of the students possessed so little natural talent that they shouldn't be allowed anywhere near a musical instrument. Ever. Yet, in order for her education to be complete, every young lady was expected to master an instrument. Such ridiculous rules were imposed upon an accomplished woman.

Two fingers pressed to her forehead, Chasity set her jaw and focused on the row of numbers in the ledger. An especially jarring screech sent talons scraping down her spine. Heaving a disgusted sigh, she set the quill aside. Slouching into the back of her chair, she glared at the door and drummed her fingertips on the chair's arms.

How was anyone supposed to get anything done with that racket going on? She'd promised Mrs. Crenshaw the finished ledgers two days ago.

Come to think of it, how did Mr. Terramier stand it, week after torturous week? Unskilled student after unskilled student? And not just here at Balderbrook's Institution for Genteel Ladies but with his other students as well?

He was no saint.

He did it for the same reasons Chasity tolerated the less pleasant aspects of her position: to put food on the table and a roof over one's head.

Though why the privileged grandson of a viscount insisted upon earning a living when the peerage looked down their illustrious noses at those who smelled of the shop, she couldn't fathom. Unless, of course, Mr. Terramier was sowing his proverbial wild oats simply to goad his family or to meet some innate drive within himself that he probably couldn't even identify. Flirtatious rapscallions like him drew women as effortlessly as the vibrant blossoms outside her office window.

Casting an envious glance to that same window, Chasity fought the urge to put aside her ledgers and sneak away for a long stroll. The day was still early enough that the temperature wouldn't be oppressive. Especially if she took a parasol.

Her favorite destination was a folly situated several yards from a pond. Trees and shrubs cocooned the stone structure on two sides, providing privacy and shade as well as homes to a variety of wildlife and birds.

Sighing and with a firm shake of her head, Chasity straightened and perused the ledger once more. As tempted as she was to throw caution to the wind and steal a few minutes for herself, she didn't dare abdicate her duties.

For the past three days, she'd felt as if she were tiptoeing on glass. From the penetrating, intense glances Mrs. Crenshaw leveled her, the headmistress had been fully informed of what had transpired during dance lessons. And Chasity would be bound that she hadn't been cast in a favorable light in the telling of the tale. Though how anyone could fault her was beyond her.

Was she supposed to be rude to Mr. Terramier in front of the students?

Wasn't she supposed to be an example to them? To demonstrate how to be a gracious and poised lady in all circumstances?

Puckering her brow, she considered Mrs. Crenshaw's behavior Wednesday. She'd seemed almost relieved that Chasity was indisposed.

Because she didn't want her near Mr. Terramier?

Something bordering on peevishness swelled behind Chasity's breastbone, though her reaction made absolutely no sense.

Perchance shutting the window would mute the cacophony occurring two doors down, and she could then concentrate on her ledgers. She'd just closed the window after another longing look outdoors and was en route to her desk when someone scratched at her office door.

Brow crinkled, Chasity slid a glance to the brass inlaid bracket mantel clock. All of the girls were in classes at the moment. The panel swung open before she'd halfway crossed the room or bid anyone entrance.

The headmistress sailed inside as if it were her right. In point of fact, it was, even if the intrusion bordered on rudeness.

"Mrs. Crenshaw?"

An irrational prickle of guilt poked Chasity. For pity's sake, she needn't feel embarrassed that Mrs. Crenshaw had found her away from her desk. Chasity entwined her fingers and stifled an apology. She'd done nothing wrong.

No doubt Mrs. Crenshaw simply wanted to review the ledgers. The *unfinished* ledgers.

Chasity resisted glancing toward her desk. "I'm afraid I haven't quite completed updating the books just yet."

There'd been quite a muddle of receipts and statements to wade through and a few confusing entries by Mrs. Crenshaw she had questions about. Likely, just as she had these past several weeks, the headmistress would shake her head and plead forgetfulness. Which meant Chasity could never quite balance the books.

Mrs. Crenshaw made a dismissive shooing motion with her hand. "I'm not here about that, though I should like to review the accounts this evening."

Her meaning was perfectly clear.

Finish the bookkeeping today.

Much easier to do if Chasity were left to the task.

She edged toward her desk.

"Can I help you?" she asked, settling into the recently vacated chair once more.

Mrs. Crenshaw had wandered to the window and gazed toward the music room. Her expression a combination of pensiveness and longing, her shoulders slumped the merest bit. In a blink, however, her ramrod straight spine was back, and her countenance was once more that of a woman in control.

Hands folded, she scrutinized Chasity's office as if she'd never been inside the room before. Or as if she was seeing it clearly for the first time.

"We have—how shall I say it?—a delicate situation, Miss Noble, and I would ask for your assistance. Naturally, I require your absolute discretion."

"Of course. I shall help if I am able."

What sort of delicate situation?

One that could cause a scandal, such as one of the girls or teachers being in the family way. If so, how had such a thing occurred? Or something far less nefarious such as a shortage of tea or sugar this month, and Chasity would be required to inform the students and instructors?

Naturally, Mrs. Crenshaw would continue to enjoy her usual portions.

Something of that nature had occurred twice this month already. Once they went without bread for five days and another week, the use of lamp oil and candles were drastically limited. In point of fact, the shortages were very odd since there should've been sufficient to last the month, given the amounts purchased.

Chasity made a mental note to recheck those figures. Occasionally, Mrs. Crenshaw also edited Chasity's entries, claiming she'd found an additional bill or receipt. Up to this point, Chasity had never questioned the headmistress. But the pattern continued, and though she couldn't put her finger on what precisely, something was off.

Quelling her impatience and suppressing the impulse to tap her toe, Chasity crossed her ankles. There was no rushing Mrs. Crenshaw. She'd get to the subject troubling her when she was well and ready.

"I've received a correspondence from Lord Woolbury." Turning her back to the window, Mrs. Crenshaw's already thin lips drew into a tight, displeased ribbon. "He's Mr. Terramier's grandfather, and he objects to his grandson teaching at Balderbrook's Institution for Genteel Ladies. His lordship is most insistent the matter be rectified at once. If I don't comply, the viscount will...make things...most *difficult*."

She chose those last words with infinite care, and Chasity had no trouble understanding what Mrs. Crenshaw didn't say. The viscount—*pompous, presumptuous prig*—had issued a threat of some sort. One that the unflappable Mrs. Crenshaw had taken to heart and which had her now pacing before the window.

No wonder Mr. Terramier had chosen to make his own way. His grandfather was an egotistical tyrant.

"I see." Chasity wasn't sure that she did, except, of course, as unfair as it was, Mr. Terramier would have to be terminated.

Mrs. Crenshaw hadn't hesitated to dismiss a pair of maids, a stable hand, and an instructor. In fact, her ability to remain coldly objective and unemotional as she turned them out was somewhat off-putting.

Chasity's stomach coiled into a tight knot when she thought of Mr. Terramier receiving his *congé* and that she wouldn't see him thrice weekly anymore.

What other solution was there, though?

Seldom were influential peers denied anything. The viscount had made his wishes known, and Mrs. Crenshaw was expected to comply with all due haste. Or suffer the threatened consequences. For assuredly, a threat had been issued, couched in the politest of terms, of course.

Chin to her chest, Mrs. Crenshaw made another stiff-legged sweep before the window. Surely, she realized there was only one recourse. Regardless, Chasity knew better than to offer advice unless Mrs. Crenshaw specifically asked for it.

"I don't believe that you do see, Miss Noble." She shook her head. "How could you?" she mumbled beneath her breath.

Indeed, how could I?

Mrs. Crenshaw's bony chest expanded as she inhaled a deep breath. She faced Chasity straight on, then said in a rush, "Mr. Terramier signed a contract to teach dance and music for one year, at which time he has the option of renewing. With an increase in wages, of course. I cannot dismiss him without cause, else, I owe him the wages he would've earned. The school does not have those funds to spare, and the viscount has insinuated he will have the school closed if I do not dismiss Mr. Terramier at once."

Chasity's jaw sagged in a wholly unrefined fashion as she gaped at the headmistress. She opened and closed her mouth twice, unable to articulate a single sound.

If Mrs. Crenshaw didn't send Mr. Terramier packing, the viscount would bring trouble down upon Balderbrook's Institution for Genteel Ladies. If she did break the contract, Mrs. Crenshaw would have to pay Mr. Terramier's wages for the remaining contract term. Ten months.

"How much is Mr. Terramier paid monthly?" Chasity asked, rapidly calculating ways to economize.

Mrs. Crenshaw had the good grace to look utterly chagrined. "Ten pounds per month."

Chasity made an inarticulate noise. She only received five-and-thirty pounds *annually*.

Was Mrs. Crenshaw off her head?

Dicked in the knob?

Had she taken to sampling the sherry too often? Why in all that was holy had she offered Mr. Terramier such a lavish contract? It was unheard of.

Chasity's own employment contract was much less lavish.

"He was reluctant to fit three partial days a week into his already busy schedule," Mrs. Crenshaw said by way of an excuse. A poor excuse, at that. "I sensed he was also disinclined to surround himself with young girls. You've seen the way they make fools of themselves, fawning over him."

Not just the students.

"I'm sure it becomes most tiresome." A distinct brittleness entered the headmistress's tenor. She didn't like other women ogling the dance instructor.

Chasity digested this bit of news. In essence, Mrs.

Crenshaw had all but bribed Mr. Terramier to take the position.

Chasity's estimation of him sank a notch.

Had Mr. Terramier manipulated the headmistress with his beguiling smile and seductive glances? Coerced the smitten woman into offering extravagant terms? Chasity hadn't thought him a charlatan or a swindler, but how well could she know him in the few hours they'd spent together—always with students present?

Her mind racing, she plucked at the fabric of her skirt hidden by her desk and considered the headmistress. She, too, chose her words with profound care.

"Those are very generous terms, Mrs. Crenshaw." Too generous, in point of fact. "I am surprised a solicitor agreed to draw them up. Perhaps there is a loophole?"

"I...I, that is..." Mrs. Crenshaw swallowed and averted her gaze. "I drew the terms up myself and also drafted the contract. I didn't want the additional expense of having a solicitor do so." She wrung her hands. Actually, wrung her hands. "Now, I don't know what to do."

Color suffused her cheeks, and pressing a hand to the juncture of her throat and collar bone, she swung her attention toward the window again.

Oh, dear Lord.

Chasity fisted the fabric of her skirt as the truth slammed into her with the force of a hurricane's winds. Mrs. Crenshaw wasn't just smitten with Aston Terramier; she was in love with him. It was pathetically obvious, and compassion sluiced through Chasity for the older woman. Her position was impossible, for Chasity was nearly positive Mr. Terramier didn't return the headmistress's regard.

Leaning forward, she placed her folded hands upon her

desk. "Forgive me, but I'm still unsure how I may be of assistance."

Casting a glance over her shoulder, the headmistress speared her with such a penetrating look, Chasity felt rather like a mouse cornered by a cat. A prickle of unease sent a shiver from her waist to her shoulders.

Pivoting slowly, Mrs. Crenshaw held Chasity's gaze. Sadness and staunch resolution etched her thin features. "Mr. Terramier *must* resign. I'm not required to pay his wages if *he* terminates our contract. At least I had the foresight to include such a clause. And a morality clause as well."

"That would be the optimal solution, I agree." Chasity gave a cautious nod. "Forgive me for being obtuse, but I still fail to see what I can do to help."

Mrs. Crenshaw had embroiled herself in this conundrum, and she would have to extract herself.

The momentary softening of the headmistress's angular features evaporated, and the in-charge, do-as-I-demand matron was fully back in place. She pointed a long, thin forefinger at Chasity.

"You, Miss Noble, are tasked with ensuring Mr. Terramier resigns. Your future at Balderbrook's Institution for Genteel Ladies depends upon it."

What? My future depends upon it?

Because Mrs. Crenshaw acted like a daft, infatuated schoolgirl and entered into a reckless and extravagant agreement, Chasity now faced possible termination? She bit the inside of her cheek to check her immediate and outraged objection. *She* was at risk of losing her position because of the headmistress's foolishness?

Nae the woman's feckless stupidity.

After inhaling a calming breath, and despite her racing

pulse, she asked, "I'm sure I'm mistaken, but your directive sounds very much like an ultimatum."

Her inscrutable countenance once more in place, Mrs. Crenshaw marched to the door.

"Call it what you will, Miss Noble. If Mr. Terramier does not give his notice, you will be terminated. I shall be required to economize sacrificially to pay him off should I be forced to sack him. I cannot ignore his grandfather's directive. I've no doubt the viscount would cause a scandal and have the doors to this school closed. That would cause harm to many more people than just yourself."

And I'm to be the sacrifice for your idiocy while you keep your position?

SIX

*Balderbrook's Institution for Genteel Ladies has hired
a new music and dance instructor. Mr. Terramier comes
thrice weekly, and I must tell you, it is problematic. He is
Lord Woolbury's grandson, and he has brought disfavor
upon the school. I sincerely believe Mr. Terramier may have
only taken to teaching to spite his overbearing grandfather.
The viscount has threatened to have the school closed. I shall
tell you all about it when I come for tea on Sunday next.*

~ Miss Chasity Noble in a letter
to Mrs. Mercy Brockman

**Balderbrook's Institution for Genteel Ladies' courtyard
That same day - late afternoon**

More grateful than he ought to have been after finishing
today's lessons, as it was his means of living, Aston made for
the school's heavy front door.

A maid tidying a flower arrangement on a hall half-table hurried forward and collected his hat from a hall tree. She extended it to him. "Here you are, Mr. Terramier."

"Thank you..." Aston had seen the perky maid a few times this last month but didn't know her name. An older maid generally greeted the guests.

"I'm Josie." She dipped into a sloppy curtsy. More of an energetic bounce, in truth. "I'm new." She scrunched her button nose. "Well, not brand new. I was hired just over a month ago. I steer clear of the dragon, lest I displease her and get sacked. She's a stickler, she is."

"Dragon?" He couldn't resist asking. "Mrs. Crenshaw?"

Josie glanced over her shoulder, then nodded and whispered, "Aye. She's all sugar and spice around you, but vinegar and piss otherwise."

"I see." Aston stifled a chuckle. He'd already deduced that about the headmistress. "Josie, may I offer you a bit of advice?"

"Of course." Eagerness shone in her pale blue eyes.

"I'd not share what you just shared with me with anyone else."

"Oh, I don't dare. Only Miss Noble." She gave a sage nod more fitting of someone several decades her senior. "She understands me."

Aston wasn't surprised the maid admired Chasity. Chasity didn't judge people and made everyone feel included. Even the frumpy instructors who were less than kind to her.

"Good day," Aston said, heartily wishing the precocious maid good luck. She'd need it if she hoped to remain employed. Either that or a muzzle because Aston didn't think she was capable of holding her tongue.

Stepping out of the building, he stretched and breathed in the clean air.

Gibney waved at him from outside the stables, and Aston returned the groom's friendly gesture. More than once, the servant had watered Aston's horse while he'd been teaching. A former soldier, the groom had been a friend to one of Mrs. Longsdon's sons.

Most servants were underpaid and overworked, and Aston made a point to pass a few coins Gibney's way every week. They'd share a few moments' conversation, but always afraid he'd lose his position, the groom hurried back to his duties.

Aston had the distinct impression Mrs. Crenshaw was quite the termagant to everyone but him. He strode across the brick courtyard to his waiting buggy. Moss grew between the red rectangular bricks under the gnarled maple trees he'd parked his buggy beneath. The trees provided shade for Roi as the faithful dog dutifully waited for Aston.

Aston rather despised Thursday lessons.

Most of the students at Balderbrook's Institution for Genteel Ladies could claim only meager musical skills. However, Adelina Fitzthistlewits was exceptionally talented and a joy to teach. Unfortunately, she'd likely never be able to use her gift beyond the occasional musical or drawing room entertainment.

Upon seeing Aston, Roi lifted his shaggy head and promptly sat up. Whining in excitement, he wagged his tail so hard, his entire hind end wiggled.

"Hello, my friend." Aston scratched behind Roi's ears, earning him a goofy, doggy grin. "Forgive me for making you wait in this heat. Mrs. Crenshaw wanted a word with me."

In truth, the conversation had been peculiar.

The headmistress had sought him out at the end of his last lesson only to ask if his tenure at Balderbrook's Institution for Genteel Ladies met his expectations. Head down, she'd paced the room, reminding him of an agitated, caged lioness he'd seen once. After he'd assured her that he had no complaints—none for her ears, at least—she'd given a stilted, distracted nod.

"Very good. Very good," Mrs. Crenshaw said, looking everywhere but at him. "I've—that is, it's been a pleasure to have you at the school."

Not exactly a reflection on his duties, but then, Mrs. Crenshaw had been acting odd of late. For about a week, to be exact. Just about as long as Miss Noble had been avoiding him. Ever since that infamous dance instruction.

What fustian rubbish.

He gave into a devilish urge to test the waters.

"I hope my performance as a dance master and a music instructor has met your expectations, Mrs. Crenshaw." Palm pressed to his chest, Aston fashioned his most disarming smile. "I would be disheartened if I've disappointed in any way."

She flushed like a green schoolgirl.

"Your, ah, performance is most satisfactory," she managed.

Bowing his head in deference, he'd said, "I'm most gratified."

"I shan't keep you." Mrs. Crenshaw made for the door but paused at the threshold, her slate blue gown swishing around her practical black shoes. She met his gaze directly then.

At her haggard appearance, shock speared Aston. Lines etched her face, purple shadows haunted her sunken eyes, and she appeared to have not slept in a fortnight.

"Thank you, Mr. Terramier. Your presence lifts one's spirits." As if she realized she'd revealed too much regarding her personal feelings, she hastily added, "Music nourishes the soul, does it not?"

"I also believe as much. Music is healing and rejuvenating."

Aston had always believed he'd acquired his love of music from his mother, a former opera singer. His father had married her against the viscount's wishes, and the dictatorial blackguard had never forgiven either of them for defying him.

Aston passed a glance over the building he'd just departed. He hadn't seen Chasity again today. Yesterday, when Mrs. Crenshaw said in passing that Chasity had a headache and had retired to her chamber, he'd suspected the fascinating blonde was avoiding him. When she'd remained conspicuously absent again today, his suspicions were confirmed.

Just as well.

So why did he, even now, skim the courtyard and meadow flanking the school's right where a quaint stone folly perched atop a knoll in search of her? There had been other weeks where he'd only seen her in passing. Why did it matter so much that since luncheon on Monday, he'd not caught a glimpse of the mesmerizing beauty?

Because something scintillating had passed between them the other day while they danced. Chasity had felt it too. But if Aston was honest with himself, he knew full well nothing could come of his attraction.

If only he could stop thinking about her.

He tossed his satchel and hat onto the threadbare seat, then picked up the leather flask that contained water. He poured a generous amount into Roi's dish, and the dog eagerly drank his fill.

"Do you need to stretch your legs before we head for home?"

Unless it was raining, Roi always enjoyed a romp. However, the dog despised the rain. Probably due to the time he'd spent on the streets, wet and miserable. While Aston taught, Roi only left the buggy long enough to relieve himself. He never explored the school's grounds unless Aston accompanied him.

"Well, come along then. Just a short walk today, I'm afraid."

Tonight, Aston dined with Theran Rutland and Constantine Kellinggrave, old school chums. They'd reconnected a few years back after bumping into each other at a musical hosted by Rutland's aunt and uncle, Lord and Lady Mumford, for their three plump daughters, amongst others.

The rather plain Mumford sisters' musical aptitude made them quite popular with their set. Though it wasn't *de rigor*, the Mumfords had insisted that as their instructor, Aston attend the gathering. He'd gained another four students as a result.

After dinner tonight, he had a business meeting with a few of his fellow investors including Bradford, Viscount Kingsley, and Roark, Earl of Clarendon. Though peers, neither made him feel inferior because he wasn't also titled.

Giving a short whistle, Aston snapped his fingers, and Roi bounded from the vehicle. He raced to the nearest bush and thoroughly watered the shrub. The dog liked to run through the meadow and chase anything that flew: insects, birds, bees, and butterflies. He'd never caught one but had a great deal of fun trying to.

As he trailed behind his dog, Aston scratched his chin. Werner had sent him a third request for funds. The letter arrived before Aston left his apartments this morning. Such persistence bespoke desperation. Aston had refused again, but curiosity had prompted him to invite his cousin to meet at the Wagging Tail Pub tomorrow.

He wasn't sure why Werner didn't just approach their grandfather about paying off his debts. Unless the viscount had cut Werner off, though that wasn't likely. He'd pay Werner's arrears and use extortion to control the pasty bugger thereafter. Which might very well be why Werner hadn't asked their grandfather for the money.

"Mr. Terramier?"

Aston half-turned, surprised but delighted to see a breathless Chasity hastily making her way toward him. Her dove gray gown trimmed in ivory bespoke reticence and style. He'd like to see her in a gown the exact shade of her eyes. Or perhaps pink or lavender. Or a rich claret red.

When he didn't immediately respond, her pretty features screwed into a puzzled frown. "Mr. Terramier?"

Coming back to himself, Aston gave her a warm smile.

"Miss Noble. A pleasure as always. Please call me Aston."

Bonnetless, she shielded her eyes from the afternoon sun. With her fair skin, she would freckle. What had been so compelling that she'd tossed off convention and sought him without the benefit of a bonnet or parasol?

"Might I have a word with you?" She swept her blue-eyed gaze around the area and stepped nearer. "Privately?"

Well, wasn't this an intriguing turn of events? "But of course."

How could he refuse such a mystifying request?

His curiosity piqued, Aston indicated the folly with a sweep of his arm. "Would the folly suffice?"

It contained five arched openings, so it wasn't strictly private. However, as no one else was about, it would do well. What was more, if Aston made sure to stand in one of the openings, no one could suggest anything untoward.

Roi chose that moment to dash back and plop his haunches in front of Chasity. Head quirked to the side and tongue lolling, he raised his right paw.

"Aren't you a dashing fellow?" she said with a lilting laugh.

Paw still raised, he gazed at her expectantly.

"He wants you to shake his paw."

She slid Aston a pleased glance and then shook Roi's paw. "It's a pleasure to make your acquaintance...?"

She looked at him again.

"Roi." Aston provided. "His name is Roi."

"Ah, I am very pleased to meet you, Your Majesty." Humor laced Chasity's words.

Naturally, she'd know his name meant king. Every teacher worth her salt spoke fluent French.

Pulling his earlobe, Aston chuckled. "I thought he deserved a noble name. I found him crouched in a doorway as a starving pup two years ago."

"He's quite the gentleman." Chasity rubbed behind Roi's ears.

Closing his eyes, Roi half groaned, half sighed in contented bliss.

"I've never had a dog," she said, retreating a step. "Not at the foundling home where I was raised, nor at either of the seminary schools I've taught at. Dogs were never permitted."

"You've missed out on a tremendous blessing then," Aston said, patting Roi's head. The dog leaned into his leg and gazed at him with adoration. "Roi is more than a pet. He's a loyal companion and a trusted friend."

"How wonderful for you," Chasity said with no hint of sarcasm but rather genuine approval. "We do have Minxy and her kittens, Tinx, Saucy, and Bubo, in Balderbrook's kitchen. She's a good mouser, and Mrs. Crenshaw hopes her kittens will be too."

Chasity wrinkled her nose in an endearing fashion. "We have rodents in the school. I don't mind the mice, but I detest the rats."

Mrs. Longsdon kept two tabbies for the same reason,

although, truth to tell, they had become pampered pets and rarely hunted.

Having had enough of human doting, Roi bounded ahead.

Aston and Chasity followed at a more sedate pace.

"Shall we step into the shade?" Aston gestured to the octagon-shaped folly atop a raised platform.

Biting her lower lip, Chasity glanced around and then nodded. "Yes, please. I forgot my bonnet, and it's rather warm."

What was so urgent she'd been compelled to toss decorum aside and pursue him?

They climbed the four wide steps and entered the cool interior through one of the arched openings. A trio of stone benches at angles to each other dominated the folly's center.

Roi ran around sniffing the interior. At one entrance, he stiffened and gave a little warning woof.

Chasity and Aston looked to where the dog stared, his tail furiously wagging.

Aston saw nothing noteworthy. Probably a squirrel or bird.

At that moment, a robin red breast took wing, and Roi barked again.

Chasity smoothed a stray strand of that spun flaxen hair off her forehead. She gazed out an opening to a pond where ducks and geese swam. "This is my favorite place on the school's lands. It's peaceful. I come here to think and pray."

"It's much like a folly on one of my grandfather's estates."

Aston had forgotten about the folly at Biddledale Park. He'd hide there when Werner had committed some sin and blamed Aston for it. He'd always be found, of course. But for a short while, there would be a reprieve from punishment.

"You had something you wished to say to me?" he encouraged. As much as he'd like to spend an idle half hour or so with Chasity, he did have a dinner engagement. Though Rutland and Kellinggrave would forgive him if he were not terribly tardy.

With her profile to him, and the afternoon sun bathing the folly, Chasity appeared angelic. Yet, furrows creased her smooth brow, and tension turned her mouth downward at the corners.

She heaved a great sigh. "Yes. I do. Something of some import, in truth."

"I'm at your disposal," Aston said.

She'd avoided him, and now she sought him out to discuss a matter that required privacy?

Chasity faced him. Hands clasped, she tilted her head to meet his gaze. "I need you to resign your post. If you do not, I shall lose mine."

SEVEN

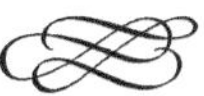

It is time for the first quarterly inspection of the new branch of Balderbrook's Institution for Genteel Ladies outlined in your duties as director and headmistress. I am aware we are nearly a month early, but Lady Balderbrook is unavailable next month Her ladyship, Mr. Bramblefink, and I shall call in the afternoon of 24 August to review the ledgers and the day-to-day operation of the London branch of Balderbrook's Institution for Genteel Ladies. Please ensure the pupils, staff, and the facility are at their very best. We wouldn't want two of the school's most generous benefactors to be disappointed in any way.

~ Mr. Pharris M. Potterburger,
in a letter to Mrs. Rafaela Crenshaw

London
Wagging Tail Pub
14 August - afternoon

Buggering sod.

Aston clenched the handle of his pewter tankard in what he feared might be a futile attempt to reign in his temper. He stretched his legs out before him on the wood floor in affected nonchalance. Werner always enjoyed getting a rise out of him, which was why Aston had learned to control his reactions as a young boy.

Giving himself a few moments to regain his composure, he disinterestedly inspected the pub. Several patrons scattered through the popular establishment spoke in low tones over foaming mugs. Others ate a simple fare of dark bread and stew. At a corner table, a pair of elderly gentlemen studied a chess-board with the intensity of generals on a battlefield. Hunched with his back to the room, a plain-clothed man scratched away at various files.

A trio of dandies dressed in the first flare of fashion entered amidst a flurry of boisterous laughter. They claimed a table in a corner and proceeded to flirt outrageously with the two pretty barmaids who rushed to their sides.

No doubt experience had taught the women that young bucks tended to tip generously after a few drinks. Come this evening, the Wagging Tail Pub would overflow with all manner of customers from lords slumming it to clerics, shop-keepers, laborers, and sailors.

Aston tapped the fingers of one hand upon the scarred tabletop. *Tappity-tap-tap. Tappity-tap-tap.* Still peeved with his cousin, he twisted his mouth into a humorless smile.

"Are you attempting to blackmail me, Werner?"

Slouching in the chair opposite Aston, Werner drained his tankard and looked around frantically for a barmaid. He raised his mug and waved it toward Marnie, the only barmaid whose name Aston knew.

She gave a saucy smile and called, "Give me a minute, guv."

"Werner?" Steel threaded Aston's voice. This little piece of horse dung thought to use extortion? "Are you?"

Werner gave a weak laugh and mopped his perspiring forehead with a handkerchief as wilted as his poorly tied neckcloth. His jacket looked in need of a good brushing too. Had he dismissed his valet?

"Of course not, Cousin," Werner dissembled. "Don't be daft."

The smile he crafted was undoubtedly meant to be reassuring, but instead, it made him appear reptilian. "I'm simply warning you that our grandfather has found brides for both of us. One good turn deserves another, don't you think?"

Aston didn't alter his stony countenance.

His grandfather knew Aston's feelings about an arranged marriage.

The bowels of hell would freeze first.

Werner cleared his throat. "If you are generous, I might be persuaded to tell you who your lucky bride-to-be is and when Grandfather plans for your nuptials to take place."

Never.

That was probably the important matter that Grandfather had demanded Aston put in an appearance for. Over his dead body.

"As I've repeatedly told you, Werner, I'm not the least inclined to be generous."

Not when the tosspot across from him had no appreciation or concept of what it meant to make one's own way in the world. Aston had never had a valet. Not even when he lived under Grandfather's roof. He'd always preferred to do things for himself.

Werner scowled, then slumped back into his chair, his chin

on a fist, resigned that no help would be forthcoming from Aston. "I thought not, but it was worth a try."

"And neither am I marrying anyone that old reprobate chooses," Aston vowed. "I owe him nothing."

"I wish I could say the same," Werner said sullenly. "Alas, it's far too late for that. Dear Grandpapa owns me body and soul, and he dashed well knows it."

A sneer skewing one side of his mouth, Werner lifted his shoulder in an I-don't-give-a-tinker's-curse insolence. It was pure artificial bravado on his part.

"Are ye both wantin' a refill then?" Marnie asked, holding up a pitcher.

"Not for me," Aston declined.

Werner pushed his mug across the table. "I do."

Ogling the tavern wench's full bosom as she refilled his tankard, Werner flicked the ruffle on her primrose yellow sleeve with his forefinger. "Up for a little fun, love?"

She eyed him with the same contempt one would a large cockroach crawling across one's dinner plate before she slid her regard to Aston. "It depends on *who* I'd be having fun with, guv," she said with a husky purr. "*Him*...or you?"

A blatant invitation if Aston had ever heard one. He hid his smirk behind the rim of his mug.

Werner's face contorted into a child's peevish glower. "Be gone with you, insolent wench. You're probably diseased anyway."

"Ye'll never know." The barmaid winked at Aston. "I bet yer bollocks are so wee, ye need a hand lens to find them."

With that insult, she sashayed away, swinging her generous hips.

"Trollop," Werner mumbled sourly into his cup.

"I thought you were particularly fond of trollops. Harlots. Bit o' muslins. Strump—"

"Shut up, Aston," Werner growled, then ducked his head when a pair of gentlemen sauntered by the window he was seated next to.

Did Werner owe them money too?

Likely, given how he was skulking like a beaten dog.

Crossing his ankle over his knee, Aston draped his arm over the back of his chair and regarded his cousin. He'd lost weight to the point of gauntness. He'd always been pale, but now his skin held a sickly greenish-ash tone.

"You don't look well, Werner. You should see a physician. I would help pay for that."

"I have," his cousin snapped. "He prescribed an elixir that sent me to the privy every ten minutes, bloody quack."

"See another then. I don't think you are well."

Werner looked quite ghastly, in truth.

"What, and have them bleed me or blow smoke up my bum like they do Father?" Werner curled his upper lip in contempt. "I'm convinced the lot of them don't know what the devil they are doing."

He might very well be right about that.

Wait. Uncle Conley is ill?

Not that the viscount would care that his only living son ailed. Conley had produced an heir, and it was Werner who would sire the next in the Woolbury line.

"Uncle is unwell?"

Werner rudely propped a scuffed booted foot atop the table, earning a glare from the tavern keeper behind the counter pouring ale and the barmaid wiping a nearby table.

"Oh, you wouldn't know about Father's decline in health, would you? You who has shunned our family these many years. Father is dying," he said with as much emotion as a butler announcing dinner.

"What's wrong with him?"

Werner lifted a shoulder. "Liver failure or something of that nature. 'Brought on by excessive drink,'" he imitated in the droll tones of an arrogant physician. "He has mere weeks left, according to the vultures Grandfather hired to treat him."

Sadness gripped Aston. He hadn't known about Uncle Conley's illness, and sympathy for the man he'd never known to be happy for a single day filled him.

"I'm truly sorry, Werner."

His cousin shrugged again and took a swallow of ale. "It makes me next in line for the viscountcy. The way Father drank, I'm honestly surprised he lasted this long," he said, no hint of affection for his sire coloring his words.

There was a great deal of truth to that statement.

Werner chuckled a drunken chortle that rattled his chest and ended in a hacking cough.

No, he was not well at all.

"Grandfather wants me married and siring heirs before the month is out. He's worried about the entailment's future. He's selected a horse-faced, long meg for me. She has a decent dowry and a nice fat trust fund." His eyes glittered greedily. "I 'spose she'll do as well as any other. I'll have to be good and foxed to bed the gel, though."

Poor woman, whoever she was. She ought to be spared such a wretched fate.

"She squints and lisps." Werner squeezed his eyes into exaggerated, mocking slits and spread his hands far apart. "And her bum is as wide as a brood cow's."

He opened one eye wide and winked. "Grandfather picked a pretty little filly for you, Saphira Finch-Hatten."

Esmerelda Finch-Hatten's sister?

Aston probed his memories. He was quite sure he'd never met her parents, either at Balderbrook's Institution for Genteel Ladies or in society.

"I wouldn't rush to say no too quickly," Werner droned on. "She's young and has a plump dowry. Not as well-bred or high in the instep as my Agatha, but a nice catch nonetheless. Naturally, as the heir, I must marry the higher-ranking woman. Agatha is the Duke of Warburton's daughter, whereas Miss Finch-Hatten's father is a mere baron."

As if Aston cared a whit about that drivel.

"As the match between you and Miss Finch-Hatten has not been formally arranged, it's not common knowledge." Werner yawned then rubbed his nape.

"It shall not be arranged," Aston snapped. He was done discussing a nonexistent betrothal.

Werner glanced nervously around the pub and, seemingly satisfied no one lurked about ready to demand immediate payment, relaxed a trifle. "I don't suppose I'll see you at my wedding? It's in a fortnight. Unless father throws a spoke in the wheel by kicking up his toes before then."

How could Werner speak so coldly and heartlessly about his father?

Aston had few memories of his parents, but they were warm and loving.

"And you cannot wait that long to pay your debts?" Aston asked, avoiding a commitment to attend. "Perhaps you can get an advance on your affianced's dowry. Or at the very least tell your creditors you'll have their funds shortly. Show them the news sheet announcement of your betrothal to hold them off if you must."

It had been done many times before by libertines and rapscallions who only saw marriage as a means to an end. And their brides as a commodity to be used for gain.

Werner grunted but remained stubbornly silent, his chin thrust out like a petulant child's.

Aston checked his pocket watch. "I have to go. I have a lesson in less than an hour."

"Ah, yes. The humble working member of our happy little family," Werner scoffed. He wiped his nose with his soggy handkerchief, then belched. "I shan't tell grandfather I've seen you. He asks me if I have all the time. You always were his favorite, even though your mother was a com—"

At Aston's darkling scowl, his cousin swiftly amended whatever he'd intended to say.

"A...commoner and mine was the daughter of a duke."

Favorite? Not by half.

Aston merely raised an eyebrow, having long ago realized Werner's jealousy was beyond his control.

"You don't deserve to know, but Grandfather is using his power and influence to discourage anyone from hiring you," Werner murmured drowsily, his head against the chair's back.

Aston paused in rising and met Werner's bleak, defeated gaze.

That cast a whole new perspective on Chasity Noble's request for him to tender his resignation at Balderbrook's Institution for Genteel Ladies yesterday. Had Grandfather threatened the school in some way?

Aston would place a wager on White's betting books he had—if Aston had a membership to the prestigious men's club. Which he neither had nor wanted.

Chasity had refused to disclose why she needed him to resign or she'd lose her position, and Aston hadn't given her a firm answer. He'd said he'd consider her request but in light of this news... Well, Grandfather would not use extortion against an innocent woman and get away with it. Though how Chasity fit into the evolving scheme, Aston hadn't deciphered yet.

"And you know this how?" he casually asked his cousin.

By now, Werner was well into his cups, and he had loose lips when foxed.

"Told me so himself. Bragged about it. Said he'd make you come 'round one way or the other." Werner suddenly sobered, his gaze penetrating and severe. "Aston, if fate decrees you to be the heir, do not let that devil's spawn succeed in his plans. You were always stronger than Father or I. Marry a woman you can love and be happy with and leave that controlling, bitter old blighter to rot."

Stunned into momentary silence, Aston stared at his cousin.

He shouldn't be surprised at the venom and acrimony Werner felt toward their grandfather. Unlike Aston, he'd never learned to forgive the man. In fairness, forgiveness was far easier to extend when one didn't have to encounter one's tormentor daily.

"Werner, is there something you're not telling me?"

Eyes shut, Werner yawned and flicked his fingers. "Don't pretend you care, Aston."

"I do care." Sometimes love demanded one take a harsh stance. "Just because I shan't do your bidding or Grandfather's does not mean I do not care."

A snore met his declaration.

Werner had succumbed to the alcohol and fallen asleep.

An insidious thought that had never once before crossed Aston's mind crept in.

What if Uncle Conley *and* Werner died?

Aston would be next in line for a peerage title he'd never wanted.

"God save me from that horror," he muttered as he left the pub.

EIGHT

I do look forward to seeing you at Mercy's for tea. Can you believe Joy and Mercy are married? Personally, I'm much like you and never entertained the notion of marrying. Toward that end, I've accepted a unique position as an amanuensis and will arrive in London, likely before you receive this letter, given the inconsistency of the post. I know you had hoped I'd accept a teaching position at Balderbrook's Institution for Genteel Ladies, but my new employer is a scholar and a scientist. I'll be transcribing his and his colleagues' notes and so forth. He doesn't mind that I'm a woman either. You know I always had an affinity for science, even though dear Mrs. Shepherd frowned upon it as being unladylike.

~ Miss Faith Roth in a note sent
to Miss Chasity Noble

Balderbrook's Institution for Genteel Ladies

Mrs. Crenshaw's office
Monday - 17 August 1818
Precisely 8:00 in the morning

Feeling very much like an errant child about to be given a scolding, Chasity sat on the edge of the uncomfortable chair situated before Mrs. Crenshaw's desk. She had no doubt the woman had picked the hard, straight-back chairs precisely because they were miserable to sit in and would discourage anyone from lingering overlong.

To the right of the blue and white porcelain inkwell and quill holder lay the stacked ledgers Chasity had finished updating late Thursday evening. She drew her eyebrows together into a minuscule frown.

Typically, the books were kept in Mrs. Crenshaw's desk drawer.

Perhaps she'd been reviewing the notes Chasity had made, inquiring about a few discrepancies as well as errors in Mrs. Crenshaw's computations before Chasity had arrived. That and the entries she simply could not read because they were so sloppily written.

She used as much tact as possible when bringing those issues to the headmistress's attention. Nevertheless, she couldn't prevent the tense knot that coiled in her stomach at this morning's summons. No one in a position of authority liked their mistakes pointed out to them by a subordinate.

Her focus fell on a closed folder before the headmistress.

Mrs. Crenshaw slipped the folder beneath the book-keeping ledgers.

"I'm sure you know why I've asked you here, Miss Noble."

Chasity swallowed but held her chin high. Mrs. Crenshaw had asked her to take on the accounting. She could not fault her for being thorough and exact.

"I believe so." Chasity's focus drifted to the ledgers. "I meant no disrespect, but I cannot reconcile the ledgers until the discrepancies are rectified."

The truth of the matter was that it had been an ongoing issue.

Mrs. Crenshaw's acrid gaze shifted to the volumes. "We can address the accounts later. I referred to your conversation with Mr. Terramier last week. I haven't received a letter of resignation from him as yet. I had anticipated a missive these past three days. Perhaps you weren't as persuasive as you might've been."

Her weak tea brown eyes burrowed into Chasity, and Chasity's stomach toppled to her toes.

She should never have been put in this utterly untenable position. Just how persuasive did Mrs. Crenshaw expect her to be, and what did coaxing constitute? For pity's sake, she'd blurted that her own employment was in peril if Aston didn't resign. She felt utterly selfish and cowardly, and it was Mrs. Crenshaw's fault.

No, it was Chasity's fault for not standing up to the headmistress.

Garnering her self-control, Chasity schooled her features.

"As I told you Thursday, Mr. Terramier said he would consider my request."

She took care to keep her tone even and calm. Honestly, he'd been remarkably civil and polite during the exchange. Much more so than she expected or deserved, in truth.

Her heart had skipped a beat when he'd said he would contemplate resigning. Part of her wanted Aston to refuse to be manipulated by Mrs. Crenshaw. Another part of Chasity genuinely feared for her position.

Mrs. Crenshaw hadn't said whether she would write Chasity a recommendation. Without one, she would be hard put to find other employment. In point of fact, respectable service would be nearly impossible to acquire.

Mrs. Shepherd could be counted on to write another recommendation, of course. Perhaps Mrs. Merilee Hornbeck, Chasity's prior headmistress, would as well. Although that would raise questions, and Mrs. Crenshaw had already proven she wasn't honest.

Chasity had no doubt that the headmistress would cast her and Aston to the proverbial wolves to save her own hide. The injustice made Chasity's blood simmer.

"I presume that means we can expect Mr. Terramier today for dance lessons?" Mrs. Crenshaw brushed a speck of dust from her glossy desktop, but she did not meet Chasity's eyes.

Yes, and ten times ten equals one hundred.

Well, it should unless Mrs. Crenshaw did the adding. Her mathematical skills were sadly lacking. How she had managed to hide that deficit during her hiring process, Chasity could not conceive. *Unless*...unless they weren't accidental but deliberate in an attempt to conceal fraud or malfeasance?

Heavens above.

What an uncharitable thought. Regardless, the seed had been planted but now was not the time to reflect upon the possibility.

"If Mr. Terramier didn't send word otherwise, I suppose we must presume he'll be here," she agreed, studying the woman across from her with new eyes.

Mrs. Crenshaw looked impossibly more fatigued than she had last week. She'd been scarce Saturday and Sunday, not even attending church with the students and instructors.

Perhaps she was ailing.

That made sense, come to think of it.

Mayhap Mrs. Crenshaw should see a physician.

Regardless, the woman's shifting the blame to Chasity for

the mess she made with Aston was reprehensible. Since Chasity had spoken with him in the folly, she'd come to think of him as Aston, rather than Mr. Terramier. It was too familiar and too forward, but as no one could see her thoughts, she indulged in the impropriety.

Those earlier suspicions Chasity had entertained about the headmistress not approving of her surfaced once more.

Was this merely a means to be rid of her?

Well, that was too bad. Chasity was made of stern stuff, and she'd not go timidly.

Lady Balderbrook and the other board members and patrons, as well as Mrs. Hornbeck, had personally selected Chasity for the position of assistant headmistress. If Mrs. Crenshaw had an issue with their choice, she could take it up with them.

Perhaps Chasity should pen a letter mentioning the irresponsible contract Mrs. Crenshaw had initiated with Aston as well as the sloppy bookkeeping. Oh, and the frequent abdication of her duties.

Prior to this, Chasity had never considered herself disloyal. Still, it was only two months into Mrs. Crenshaw's directorship of this branch of Balderbrook's Institution for Genteel Ladies, and Chasity had severe concerns about the headmistress's competency. Surely the board and benefactors ought to be made aware.

But did that make Chasity a traitor?

No. Not in the least. It made her responsible and ethical amid a complicated situation. It wasn't only her position precariously hanging in the balance either.

What about the other instructors?

Come to think of it, funds had been provided to hire two additional teachers. Was Mrs. Crenshaw spending those monies too?

If so, that certainly explained why she'd turned down every single applicant thus far.

Was the headmistress also an embezzler?

Yes, Chasity's obligation to the school, her fellow instructors, and the students surpassed her loyalty to Mrs. Crenshaw. Something was too smoky by far, and it was time to investigate just what in the world was going on.

"You shall have to speak with him again today, Miss Noble."

No. I shan't.

Lord, give me patience and bridle my tongue.

Chasity shoved her musings aside and directed her full attention to the headmistress. Clenching her hands in her lap, she curled her toes into her shoes until they cramped.

"I cannot do that. Mr. Terramier said he would consider the suggestion." Chasity believed Aston would. He'd appeared genuinely shocked and concerned at her declaration. "Perchance, Mrs. Crenshaw, he would be more influenced to acquiesce if you were to ask him to resign."

"No!"

One sharp, unrelenting syllable.

Mrs. Crenshaw fashioned the merest upward turn of her mouth. "What reason could I possibly give? His work is exemplary. And I fear a court would consider me asking him to leave the same as terminating him." Her face fell. "Pray God it does not go that far. It must not."

Chasity was no solicitor, but surely a voluntary separation of employment was not the same as dismissal. However, she ceded Mrs. Crenshaw's point. If the matter were to go before a magistrate—*would Aston go that far?*—Mrs. Crenshaw's tenure as director was over.

In point of fact, Chasity was beginning to think that may not be such a bad thing.

"By the by," Mrs. Crenshaw said, abruptly changing the subject. "We are to have guests Wednesday. Mr. Potterburger, Mr. Bramblefink, and Lady Balderbrook will join us on the twenty-fourth for the first quarterly inspection."

More than a month early.

She looked positively ill as she imparted that news. She raised a shaky hand and pressed her fingers to her forehead.

"I have a persistent headache," she offered by way of an explanation.

"Shall I have Cook prepare a powder for you?" Chasity refused to let her attention glide to the ledgers or the partially visible folder beneath them. It looked suspiciously like a personnel folder.

Chasity's?

Aston's?

"No. No. That shan't be necessary." Mrs. Crenshaw waved toward the tea tray atop a locked cabinet. "I'll have a cup of tea. It always works wonders."

"How shall I prepare for Lady Balderbrook and the others?" Chasity asked.

She didn't begrudge the headmistress her tea tray. The woman had not joined the staff for breakfast for the fourth day in a row. Nevertheless, Chasity had noticed the expensive assortment of dainties and sweets, which no one else was ever offered.

Mrs. Crenshaw slid a piece of foolscap across the desk. "I've taken the liberty of making a short list."

Chasity glanced at the neat rows of script. Nothing out of the ordinary. Except the distinct difference in penmanship between this note and the bookkeeping ledgers in Mrs. Crenshaw's hand.

The school's doors had only been open for a short while. The benefactors would understand things weren't running tip-top quite yet due to the shortage of instructors. Still, the staff was efficient, the building and grounds well-maintained and tidy, and Chasity was confident the students would be on their best behavior.

"Very good. I shall attend to this at once." Half expecting Mrs. Crenshaw to waylay her, she rose and folded the list. 'Now, I must get to my class."

She would be late if she didn't hurry.

"I cannot supervise dance instructions today." The head-mistress drew one of the school's ledgers before her. "I have much to do to prepare for the inspection."

What a surprise. Coward.

"Of course." Which meant Chasity had to face Aston after asking him to resign. How utterly selfish he must think her. Asking him to give up his livelihood so that she could keep hers.

Remorse's claw-like feet tiptoed across her shoulders.

She'd allowed fear to dictate her behavior and, in doing so, had compromised her integrity. Come what may, she would apologize and retract her request. If Mrs. Crenshaw wanted Aston gone, she'd have to see to the unpleasant task herself.

"Should I ask him to dine with us?" That had become customary. However, Chasity wasn't going to presume as much. Hopefully, she'd find the opportunity to express her regret to him—not readily done with nearly fifty girls underfoot.

"Why, yes." Was that a speculative gleam in the head-mistress's eyes? "Although, I don't believe I'll be finished going over the books by then. This is the first opportunity I've had to review the accounts."

She hadn't even looked at Chasity's notes yet?

Well, Mrs. Crenshaw had best get on it if the books were

to be balanced before the twenty-fourth. Chasity gave her a long look. Was she going to own up to her responsibility?

Finally?

After donning her spectacles, Mrs. Crenshaw opened the first ledger. "You'll have to take my place as hostess for luncheon."

Hardly the hostess and Chasity was quite becoming used to taking the headmistress's place.

"As you wish," Chasity said with a slight nod.

As she slipped from the room, she couldn't help but feel a sense of foreboding.

NINE

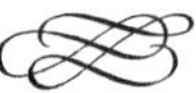

*As you are unattached, the other investors and thought
perhaps you'd enjoy a trip to our marble quarry in Italy.
Naturally, all expenses would be covered if your schedule
permits the journey. If you are interested, we can discuss the
details when the investors next meet. We anticipate a trip
of at least a month, perhaps more.*

~ Bartholomew Yancy, Earl of Ramsbury,
in a letter to Aston Terramier

Balderbrook's Institution for Genteel Ladies
20 August - almost noon

Snapping his violin case closed upon the settee, Aston glanced
up when he heard a sharp tap on the window facing the
gardens. Her blue eyes wide and worried, Chasity peered
inside, reminding him of a precocious child. After hastily

looking behind her shoulder, she made a frantic motion for him to open the window, and he grinned.

In a few strides, he reached the window and drew it open.

"Well, hello. To what do I owe this honor?" he quipped, leaning a shoulder against the jamb and folding his arms.

Did she intend to ask him to resign again?

He hoped not because Aston still hadn't decided what he was going to do. The subject wasn't far from his thoughts, yet Chasity's request didn't make sense. He needed more information. Assuredly he wouldn't give his blasted grandfather the satisfaction unless it was for an extraordinary reason.

What didn't make sense at all was Chasity getting sacked if he didn't resign.

How could the two possibly be connected?

Aston had no doubt Mrs. Crenshaw had put Chasity up to it, and any previous compassion or empathy he'd held for the woman disintegrated. What a cowardly, despicable thing to do, and Aston believed he knew why she'd taken the particular tack she had.

Mrs. Crenshaw didn't want to pay the balance of his wages if she terminated him without cause. As she couldn't dismiss him for fault, she was good and stuck.

Had he suspected the headmistress had acted outside of her authority by offering him the generous contract, he never would've accepted. Particularly after she'd become overly friendly toward him, but blister it all, he would *not* let his grandfather triumph in his separation from Balderbrook's Institution for Genteel Ladies.

Which was the primary reason he couldn't decide about the trip to the Italian marble quarry he had invested in either. He'd dreamed of traveling to Italy, and since the expenses were paid, he ought to jump at the opportunity.

"Hurry, help me inside."

Chasity hoisted a very shapely white stockinged leg which, in turn, flowed into a well-turned ankle over the sill and, with an unladylike grunt, hefted herself onto the ledge. She dangled there, half inside and half outside, looking quite like an impish child on a seesaw.

She scowled.

"A little help, Aston?"

Aston, is it?

Chuckling, he scooped her into his arms. "Wouldn't the door have been far easier?"

He glanced toward the panel, startled to realize his last pupil hadn't shut it tightly. The door stood open a couple of inches. He couldn't see anything of the corridor and doubted anyone could see him and Chasity either. Especially if he drew her farther into the L-shaped alcove where the students practiced.

She gave him an arch look. "It would've been. But someone also might've seen me enter, and propriety dictates I leave the door wide open, which would defeat my purpose."

"Because you want to be alone with me?" Aston waggled his eyebrows, his nose a mere inch from hers. "That sounds most intriguing," he teased.

The silver specks in her eyes sparkled with embarrassment and awareness. Her face aflame, she demanded, "Put me down, Aston."

He complied at once, holding her shoulders until she'd steadied herself, then he retreated a pace.

Chasity smoothed her forest green skirts with long elegant fingers. An ink smudge stained her right thumb. Her color still high, but oh so delightfully endearing, she heaved a large breath. "I've been trying to catch you alone for days."

"Indeed? Why might that be?" he purred, adoring how easily he could fluster her. "I am flattered."

"You needn't be," she said crisply.

Her expression vacillated between apprehension and chastisement. And if Aston didn't miss the mark—and he was quite certain he hadn't—feminine interest.

Chasity wasn't here because she found him irresistibly charming or had desired a private *tête-à-tête* with him. He'd wager she was here at Mrs. Crenshaw's behest again.

He braced himself for her request, disappointed she'd do Mrs. Crenshaw's bidding. But then, he wasn't in Chasity's position and didn't have to depend upon the seminary for his entire livelihood as she did. Still, he'd believed Chasity more of an independent soul—a woman of substance and gumption and one who knew her own mind.

She gave him a sideways look. "You haven't joined us for luncheon."

It wasn't an accusation but a statement of fact.

"I thought it wiser not to."

Aston couldn't sit beside Mrs. Crenshaw and pretend all was well when the scheming shrew had threatened Chasity.

Straightening her turned-up cuff, Chasity gave a slow nod.

"I have to agree. I was prepared to send a note to your residence asking you to meet me somewhere private. Most inconveniently, Mrs. Crenshaw keeps her office locked, so I couldn't look through your employee file to find your address. I was reduced to skulking around outside windows."

She gave the still open window a pointed look.

Now it was her turn to jest, and he chuckled, recalling the very proper Miss Noble straddling the window sill with her gown rucked to delectably dimpled knees.

"I'm delighted you came skulking," he said with a devilish grin.

That earned him a pale eyebrow raised in reprimand.

Aston glanced at the clock and drew his brows together.

"You'd best hurry and tell me what it is you need to say. It's nearly time for luncheon, and I don't want you to risk further disfavor with Mrs. Crenshaw."

Or the other instructors who reminded him of ill-tempered hens ready to peck and poke at an easy target. In this case, Chasity because she was young and pretty, and they weren't.

"Ah, about that..." Chasity pressed fingers to the bridge of her nose for a moment.

She slanted her head to meet his eyes, and his breath stalled somewhere behind his ribs.

She was bold and brave and beautiful.

"I want to apologize, Aston. Asking you to resign was dishonorable and beneath me. I am ashamed and embarrassed. I have no excuse except that I let fear spur me on. Please forgive me. I do not want you to resign. I feel like I have a friend in you—the only friend I have here."

She looked so sincere, her dark blue eyes round and her pink lips slightly parted. Aston had not blamed her for her part in Mrs. Crenshaw's ill-hatched scheme. Chasity was a victim, whether she realized it or not.

Aston's attention gravitated to her mouth again.

He wanted to kiss her. Never mind that there was nothing the least romantic or arousing in her apology. If he were honest with himself, he'd wanted to kiss her since that day he'd waltzed with her. Chasity affected him as no other woman ever had. She made him want things he'd never desired before. Things he thought to never have.

A home. A wife. Children.

Those were for other people.

Not for him.

Never for him.

He'd never subject his wife or children to his grandfather's evil machinations. For that is exactly what would happen. That's what he'd done to Aston's parents and to Uncle Conley. Aston's unpleasant musings must've reflected in his countenance because Chasity regarded him with a hint of wariness.

And yet, she stood there waiting for his reaction, not knowing if he'd be angry or belligerent or offended.

"Aston?"

Aston closed the distance between them and placed his hands on her delicate shoulders. "You are forgiven, completely and absolutely. Think no more on it. It's as if it never happened."

"Thank you." She closed her eyes for a moment, the lashes fanning her high cheekbones.

If only he had the right to draw her against his chest and comfort her. To assure her that he'd make everything right.

"Chasity, I know you wouldn't have entertained the notion if your situation weren't dire. I wish you'd tell me what is going on. Why you are afraid. What hold does Mrs. Crenshaw have over you?"

To his horror, tears welled in Chasity's indigo eyes, and her lower lip trembled.

"Don't cry, sweetheart." Aston did draw her into his arms then. How could he not? "I'll help in any way I can. Tell me, what has you so distressed so that I can."

She shook her head, releasing a whiff of lemon and flowers.

"I'm not sure exactly. All I do know is that your grandfather has threatened to close the school down. He doesn't want you teaching here."

Chasity confirmed what Aston had suspected since speaking with Werner. Grandfather was exercising his aristocratic muscles to manipulate again.

"Mrs. Crenshaw said if I didn't persuade you to give up your post voluntarily, she'd sack me and use my salary to help pay off her contractual obligations to you."

The jealous hag.

The headmistress would give Chasity her *congé* for no legitimate cause other than a trumped-up excuse to confiscate her wages?

"I suspect she's been looking for a reason to sack you, Chasity."

No authentic reason, that was certain.

"I've speculated as much myself," she mumbled into his shirt as he caressed her slender back. "She has no basis, and so she must devise something underhanded."

Up and down. Up and down, he moved his hands in soothing motions.

"Shh," Aston comforted. "Don't fret. We'll work something out."

What or how, he didn't know.

Aston kissed the crown of Chasity's head, savoring the bliss of embracing her. He longed to do much, much more. This woman had come to mean far too much to him these past weeks. He had no right to hold her in his arms and wish for things that could never be.

"Mrs. Crenshaw said she needed my salary to offset the cost of paying off your contract. But there is still funding budgeted for two other instructors yet to be hired."

"I fear she's jeopardizing the school, the staff, and the students." Chasity angled her head back, her lashes spikey from her tears. Her eyes searched his, reaching to the depths of his soul and tugging something loose there. Something only she was capable of stirring. Freeing.

Aston yearned to kiss away every vestige of her tears and reassure her that everything would be fine.

"How can she be so short of funds when we only opened our doors two months ago?" she asked, her forehead furrowed in consternation. She caught her lower lip between her teeth and shook her head.

"I honestly don't know," he replied sincerely.

And Aston didn't.

His intuition fairly screamed something nefarious was afoot, and Chasity had been caught in the crossfire through no fault of her own. Lord, how he wanted to protect her. Shield her from whatever was going on. To ensure she didn't lose her position.

There was only one way to do the latter.

Quit.

Aston must resign his post.

And let Grandfather win?

So that he could lord it over Aston? Pour salt in the wound? Gloat that he'd finally succeeded in bending Aston to his will?

The very idea set his blood to boiling.

But for Chasity... *She* was the only reason he'd even consider it.

Of its own volition, Aston's attention dropped to Chasity's plump mouth. Her lips were full and pink. So tempting and sweet. So kissable.

What would she taste like?

Tea? Lemon? Honey?

Chasity?

"Next week, board members and benefactors, including Lady Balderbrook, are arriving to conduct the first quarterly inspection," she said, absently tracing his lapel with a fingertip. "Per Mrs. Crenshaw's request, I keep the school's books, though she still makes entries too. I've found a number of... *incongruities* in the account ledgers."

That brought Aston's carnal musings up short.

"Incongruities?" Hands braced on her slender shoulders, he leaned back, searching her face.

She nodded. "Irregularities. Mislabeled entries. Wrong amounts. Double or triple entries. But she always has a reasonable excuse."

"Do you think Mrs. Crenshaw is guilty of wrongdoing or simply sloppy bookkeeping?" He hesitated to say embezzling or stealing funds. Those were serious charges.

Chasity peered up at him, her clear gaze full of trust.

"I want to believe it's the former. But I..." She blinked and dropped her focus to his neckcloth. "I am loath to say it aloud. But I'm not convinced anymore that it's not the latter."

Neither was Aston.

Glancing up again, she skewed her mouth sideways. "It's become frequent and serious enough that I've considered notifying the board or the benefactors about my concerns."

A strangled gasp had them both pivoting toward the doorway.

Fiend seize it.

Mrs. Ramsbottom stood on the threshold, one hand clutching her throat and the other bracing herself on the frame.

Behind her, Josie froze mid-step. She had also heard Chasity's last words. Her attention careened from Aston to Chasity to Mrs. Ramsbottom and then to Aston again. Swallowing, she darted a wary glance behind her and then fled.

Chasity made an inarticulate noise of distress.

From Mrs. Ramsbottom's thunderstruck expression, she'd heard more than she ought to have done. The question was, what precisely would she do with the information?

TEN

I do not mean to complain. I am grateful for my position and know how fortunate I am. But Mrs. Crenshaw has me performing most of her duties as well as my own. I have also come into some information regarding her honesty and integrity that greatly concerns me. These findings are such that I believe the benefactors and board ought to be made aware. She's already threatened me with dismissal, and yet I must not let my personal fears guide me. I must stand on the godly principles I was raised upon and do what is right, even if the cost is most dear to me.

~ Journal entry by Miss Chasity Noble
Said journal is hidden beneath
a loose board in the wardrobe

London, England
Grosvenor Square, Mayfair

Pelandale House
Half-past three in the afternoon
23 August 1818

"Whatever are you going to do if you get sacked?" Her features pleated with concern, Mercy Brockman laid her hand atop Chasity's, which rested upon her knee, and gave a reassuring squeeze.

I honestly don't know.

And Chasity didn't.

In her mind, she'd been around and around the possible scenarios, and none ended well, except Mrs. Crenshaw's removal as director and headmistress. But as Chasity was beginning to discern, Mrs. Crenshaw was exceptionally crafty and cunning.

Their cooling tea had been forgotten on the mahogany pillar tea table. The four friends huddled together in the Marquess and Marchioness of Trenholm's stately drawing room and discussed Chasity's predicament in hushed tones.

The small gathering for tea Mercy had promised Chasity had grown to a mere fifty or sixty of London's loftiest. Undoubtedly, there were thrice as many *le bon ton* who hadn't made the cut and, even now, discussed their disfavor with others equally disgruntled about their lack of invitation.

However, this animated throng provided Chasity and her friends the perfect opportunity to sequester themselves in a quiet corner for a coze. The four women hadn't all been together since they'd lived at Haven House and Academy for the Enrichment of Young Women before any of them took their first paid positions.

Chasity had seized upon Mercy's invitation to tea as an opportunity to escape the school for a few short hours. Balderbrook's Institution for Genteel Ladies no longer felt safe or welcoming. Since Thursday, she'd waited tense and alert, fearing that at any moment Mrs. Crenshaw would lower the proverbial hammer and boot Chasity to the curb for an imagined or contrived infraction.

"It's so blasted wrong," Faith Roth said vehemently, her strawberry blonde eyebrows veering sharply together. "Why should you be punished for being honest?"

"I'm praying it shan't come to anything as extreme as my dismissal," Chasity admitted.

"And I truly hope that I am mistaken in my suspicions."

She'd had time to reflect these past days and had come to the disquieting conclusion that she was not. Mrs. Crenshaw had entered too many convenient *errors* in the books.

At the very least, the headmistress should be dismissed for her ineptitude and incompetence. At the worst...charged with embezzlement, misappropriation, and malfeasance, which would undoubtedly mean imprisonment.

The good Lord only knew what Mrs. Crenshaw might be capable of in order to hide her crimes. Look what she'd asked of Chasity in order to manipulate Aston?

Yes, indeed, Chasity must be extremely careful and prudent until the matter was resolved.

"We shall all pray that it doesn't," Joy Morrisette avowed, leaning in and nudging Chasity's shoulder with her own. "I can ask my husband if he has heard of any positions should it come to that. Brandon knows a great many people, and they are always confiding in him."

"I've already written Lady Balderbrook, requesting a private audience with her tomorrow when she comes for the quarterly inspection." Chasity almost feared revealing that secret, except these were her dearest friends. They'd been raised together as sisters. She could trust them.

Mrs. Crenshaw was sure to fly into a dither or have an

apoplexy if Lady Balderbrook honored Chasity's request and met with her privately. However, Chasity would tackle that obstacle if and when it arose.

"At this juncture, all I can do is pray her ladyship indulges me." Chasity gave a little shrug. "Or else I'll have no recourse but to write letters to the board members and reveal my suspicions."

Perhaps she ought to pen the letters tonight and stash them someplace safe if she was dismissed. She might not have convenient or immediate access to ink and a quill wherever she found herself if she was terminated from Balderbrook's Institution for Genteel Ladies.

Yes. Yes. That was precisely what she would do.

She supposed she could always return to Haven House and Academy for the Enrichment of Young Women for a time. Although if her reputation were soiled, she might bring disgrace upon the girls still at the foundling home and make it difficult for them to find employment.

Well then, Chasity would have to do everything in her power to ensure she kept her position. She knew exactly what her contract terms were, and she hadn't committed any act worthy of termination. Being truthful was neither immoral nor an act of insubordination. Neither was it disloyal, as no supervisor or employer had the right to request or require someone to be deceitful.

If Mrs. Crenshaw thought Chasity would go quietly without a fight, she had better devise another scheme. To Chasity's knowledge, Stella Ramsbottom hadn't shared the conversation she'd overheard between Chasity and Aston with Mrs. Crenshaw.

Or had Stella been deliberately eavesdropping?

Most likely.

From the conspiratorial covert glances Pomposa Wetherwax and Geraldine Belcher had leveled Chasity the past two days, Mrs. Ramsbottom *had* blathered what she'd heard to them.

Why she hadn't snitched to Mrs. Crenshaw yet, Chasity had no idea.

Yesterday when cleaning the hearth in Chasity's office, Josie had confided, "I would have my tongue cut out before I betrayed you, miss. Your secret is safe with me."

"Thank you, Josie." She truly was a dear thing.

Josie had edged closer, and after a furtive glance around the room only the two of them occupied, had whispered, "I always knew there was something off about the headmistress. My mum always says if something seems fishy, you can bet it will start stinking soon enough."

Chasity wasn't exactly sure what that was supposed to mean, but she had no reason to doubt Josie's sincerity.

Mercy's gaze circled the room before she focused on Chasity once more and offered an encouraging upward sweep of her mouth. Mercy jutted her chin out. She'd always had a mulish bend.

"We're departing for the country early tomorrow morning, but I shall ask Ronan if you might stay with us," she said matter of factly. "There is plenty of room. Before you leave today, I'll give you the direction to Kelvingrove Park."

"You'll do no such thing. I'm not about to impose upon a newly married couple."

Chasity tempered her reply with a brave smile. The notion rather horrified her, in truth. Besides, this house wasn't Mercy's. It was her in-laws. They might feel entirely different about a stranger in their midst.

"However, I would appreciate it if you could find a position for a capricious housemaid who has been a loyal friend to me," Chasity said. "I'm afraid she won't last at Balderbrook's even if I do."

"Consider it done," Mercy assured her with the confidence of one who knows her husband and family would support her decision. "She can inquire here. I'll leave a note with the butler."

In recent days, doubt had begun to niggle in the back of Chasity's mind, and she wasn't positive she wanted a life as an instructor or assistant headmistress anymore. Just because she was an excellent teacher didn't mean she found joy in it. The truth of it was, she'd been perfectly content with her lot in life until a certain dance master had come upon the scene.

"I'm so sorry you are going through this, dearest." This from Faith as Joy and Mercy nodded in agreement.

They mightn't share any blood, but they'd always been like sisters.

Mercy glanced up, and a rosy blush suffused her cheeks, causing all of the women to look to where she stared. Her husband, Ronan Brockman, grinned at his new wife, then gave her a decidedly wicked wink.

"He's a complete rapscallion," Mercy said with such love that it was obvious she meant it as a compliment.

Chasity was glad for her friend.

Mercy had found love. Something women born into their stations weren't always permitted. She exchanged a knowing glance with Faith, who, like Chasity, had never imagined herself married. However, an irregular twinge somewhere behind her breastbone forced Chasity to confront that tarradiddle.

She'd never imagined marriage before meeting Aston. How one man could disrupt her well-ordered life and make her want something she'd always disdained made no sense.

Security and stability had always been at the forefront of every decision she made. Every goal she'd set and attained.

Women could not afford to be without either. Life was cruel to those unfortunate women.

Had Chasity's mother been one of those wretches?

A female who'd been a victim of her circumstances?

Chasity would never know.

Eager to change the subject, she picked up her teacup and took a sip of delicious, if tepid, tea. "I wish Purity could've joined us today. She wrote and said it's likely her charges will all be off to boarding schools soon. I hope she applies for one of the open positions at Balderbrook's..."

Her voice trailed off.

A helpless feeling overcame her. If she weren't there, there wasn't a snowball's chance in a bonfire Mrs. Crenshaw would hire any friend of Chasity's.

Joy must've sensed her distress because she plastered a brilliant smile upon her face and said, "Tell us about your new position, Faith."

Faith grinned, the freckles on her face seeming to take on a life of their own. "I start tomorrow." Excitement fairly oozed off of her. "At first, I shall only transcribe for Lord Kellinggrave. He's the third son of a duke, but—"

She stopped speaking abruptly and blinked her big brown eyes rather owlishly behind her spectacles.

"Why, that's him. Lord Constantine Kellinggrave," she reiterated for their benefit. "There, the tall blond wearing a gray jacket that just entered the drawing room with that dark-haired gentleman."

Chasity turned her head, and her gaze snared with Aston's. He swept his gaze over her, wrapping her in deep brown velvetiness. Her tummy fluttered most irregularly.

What was he doing here?

Naturally, it wasn't preposterous that he'd be invited or know someone who'd been invited. Aston was a viscount's grandson, after all. No doubt, he was well acquainted and associated with many of those present today as well as others amongst the *haut ton*.

Chasity only knew her friends and just today had been introduced to Dr. Brandon Morrisette, Joy's husband, and Lord Ronan Brockman, Mercy's new husband. That she'd recognized Lady Finch-Hatten and her daughter Saphira upon her arrival didn't count.

Lady Finch-Hatten's other daughter attended Balderbrook's Institution for Genteel Ladies, but Chasity wasn't foolish enough to attempt to greet the woman. Her ladyship had turned her frosty gaze upon Chasity and regarded her with the same revulsion one would fresh horse manure in the parlor.

Aston said something to Lord Kellinggrave, who glanced toward the women. His astute green gaze rested on each of the ladies for a moment before gliding away as a rotund dame swathed in a shocking shade of pink and wearing a gold and fuchsia turban from which poked three peacock feathers demanded his attention.

A rueful smile quirking one side of his mouth, his lordship bowed. However, before he'd completely straightened, the zealous woman grabbed his arm with the tenacity of a terrier seizing a rat in its jaws. Kellinggrave murmured something to Aston and received a nod in response.

Talking the whole while, the vivacious matron towed Lord Kellinggrave across the room.

Nothing in his bland expression had indicated he'd recognized Faith. For Lord Kellinggrave to have passed her over as if they'd never met, he must indeed be every bit the absent-minded scholar Faith had described him to be.

Chasity slid her friend a quick, sympathetic glance. No one liked to be invisible or to be disregarded.

The two lines wrinkling the bridge of Faith's nose revealed she'd noticed her new employer's obvious lack of acknowledgment. She cut him a sideways look and narrowed her eyes the merest bit at his broad back.

She wasn't pleased.

Faith had no trouble speaking her mind, and Chasity suspected Lord Kellinggrave might very well get an earful tomorrow. Chasity would rather like to observe that exchange. She had no doubt who would come out the victor.

A grin threatened, and Chasity returned her attention to Lord Kellinggrave. His lordship was now deep in conversation with two fusty-looking, doddery fellows as well as the dame.

Aston's long strides had carried him halfway across the drawing room already.

Chasity forced herself to look away as he approached, lest her friends see her acting like a calf-eyed nincompoop. He was the seminary's dance master and music teacher. She was the assistant headmistress. *For now.* That was all.

"That's him," she said out the side of her mouth to no one in particular. "Aston Terramier."

As one, her three friends trained their inquisitive gazes upon him.

Couldn't they have tried to be even a mite subtler?

Chasity almost groaned with the humiliation assaulting her.

They weren't the only ones boldly staring at Aston either.

Astonishment momentarily held her immobile when something very much like jealousy rose in her breast as several young, polished, and perfumed young ladies hungrily took Aston's measure. One with the predatory glint of a tigress in her hazel eyes brazenly licked her lower lip before whipping her fan open.

A pretty doe-eyed brunette went pale as chalk when an older woman greatly resembling her harshly whispered something in her ear. Probably her mother. Whatever she'd said to her daughter had the poor girl shrinking into the corner where they stood with her attention rooted to the Aubusson carpet.

Aston wore a finely-tailored black suit, a royal blue striped waistcoat, and a crisp white cravat. He was breathtaking. He looked every bit the fine gentleman, despite his slightly too long hair curling over his collar and his nose, which was a trifle too strong to be considered fashionable.

Chasity wore her finest gown, a simple ivory affair adorned with pink ribbons that didn't begin to compare with the elegant frocks adorning the ladies of quality. She even lacked matching slippers, and her simple black shoes covered her feet.

For the first time in her life, she yearned for a stunning gown with matching slippers and ribbons threaded through her perfectly coiffed curls. Perhaps even a pendant and earrings to complete the ensemble.

She'd been raised to value inner beauty and not fallalls and fripperies. However, the truth was she wouldn't mind a few fancy outward adornments if they made her attractive to Aston.

"He's quite dashing for a dance master," Joy whispered. "And tall too."

"And to think, we had to settle for short, decrepit Monsieur Paternoster," Mercy said with a mischievous twinkle in her eye. "He limped and always smelled of garlic and camphor."

"I might've actually learned to enjoy dancing if our instructor looked anything like your Mr. Terramier, Chasity." Faith almost choked on a teasing giggle.

"Hush. All of you. He's not *my* Mr. Terramier." Chasity gave them a mockingly stern gaze. "I had no idea he'd be here."

Having made it to their table, Aston bowed. "Miss Noble. What a pleasant surprise to see you today."

In short order, Chasity introduced her friends to Aston. "We all attended the same academy."

The women raised and educated at Haven House and Academy for the Enrichment of Young Women didn't speak about the very private home. Only Hester Shepherd knew the origins of the girls in her charge. The girls didn't even know, although Mercy had discovered who her mother was. Because Mercy and Lady Amhurst looked so much alike, anyone with eyes in their heads could see the resemblance and rightly conclude the obvious familial relationship between the women.

Whoever chose to leave a girl at the foundling home paid a fortune for Mrs. Shepherd's discretion. The upper ten thousand liked to keep their many skeletons well hidden in their lavish closets.

"Might I have a word with you, Miss Noble?" Aston asked with one of his disarming smiles. The one that turned bones to jelly and caused a hoard of butterflies to take wing in one's stomach.

"Indeed." Mercy quickly rose. "Come along, Faith and Joy. I haven't shown you the roses yet. They are my mother-in-law's pride and joy."

Before Chasity could object, Mercy had bid Aston a polite, "Please excuse us," and bundled the other two women away.

Mercy glanced around the room, uncomfortably aware of the eyes trained on her and Aston. As they were in full view of dozens of people, no one could object to his speaking to her alone. Except that she was a commoner, and he was an aristocrat. There was always that little detail that stuck in the craw of a good many in the peerage.

Aston sank onto the settee beside Chasity, angling his back to provide a barrier against the curious onlookers. "I've decided to resign my position at Balderbrook's Institution for Genteel Ladies next month. I've been given the opportunity to go to Italy on business."

ELEVEN

Your uncle is dying. He shan't last the night. Have the good grace and decency to pay your last respects. Not for my sake, for I know that won't sway you, but for Conley's. He asks for you.

~ Viscount Woolbury in an urgent message
to Aston Terramier
Sent by messenger in the late afternoon
of Sunday, 23 August 1818

Trentholms' drawing room
Several stilted tick-tocks of the longcase clock later

Aston had meant to tell Chasity of his decision on Monday, but there was no sense making her wait for the good news. He thought she'd be overjoyed, but her crestfallen expression said otherwise. As was her wont, her mask of professionalism slid into place before he took another breath.

"That sounds like an intriguing adventure, Mr. Terramier. I wish you well."

Ah, back to Mr. Terramier, was she?

Chasity was mindful of the ears flapping nearby.

She was an absolute vision today. This was the first time Aston had ever seen her wear anything but dark, somber shades. The light gown with its pretty pink ribbons suited her. She should always wear pastel colors. They enhanced her ethereal beauty.

Unfortunately, somber hues were expected of instructors at girls' seminaries.

He firmed his mouth and cast a glance behind him. Too many people eyed them beneath their lashes or from the corner of their eyes. A few of the bolder and more intrusive, stared outright.

"Dash it all. That's not the reason I'm tendering my resignation," Aston insisted, taking care to lower his voice. "It's so that you can keep your position. I'll still be thwarting my grandfather's plans to boot."

She angled her head, the sunlight behind her bathing her in a golden halo. Her gaze searched his face, and a hint of something—*pity*?—darkened her eyes to navy-blue.

Her tone equally subdued, she asked, "Is that what motivates all you do? Thwarting your grandfather?"

"Of course not," Aston responded automatically and not a little defensively.

Her questions abraded his conscience.

Isn't it?

No. Of course it wasn't.

"I shall miss you. Truly. Balderbrook's shan't be the same without you." Chasity fashioned a sad little half-smile. "If I manage to stay on as assistant headmistress, that is."

Aston intended to assure that as a condition of his voluntary resignation. Chasity would be guaranteed her position. And he'd get it in writing. Mrs. Crenshaw could not dismiss

Chasity for any reason except a blatant immoral or criminal act.

Peering past him, Chasity toyed with the ribbon at her trim waist. There was an ink stain on her thumb. She brought her attention back to him. "I cannot help feel remorse and guilt that you won't be there, and it is partially my fault."

"I don't hold you accountable at all." Aston needed to speak with her alone. Where neither of them feared eavesdroppers. "I've devised a plan."

She raised a dubious eyebrow. "A *plan?*"

Such skepticism weighted those two small words, he made a sound near a frustrated growl in his throat. He must tell her his tactics before tomorrow when he intended to speak with Mrs. Crenshaw. Before the board came for their inspection. He also planned to have a word with the board members and ask that they investigate the headmistress, though Chasity didn't need to know that.

Bollocks to propriety.

Aston took her hand and pulled her to her feet. "Come with me."

"Where to?" Chasity peered past his shoulder and paled slightly. "People are staring at us. I don't wish to draw attention."

Too late for that.

Chasity's beauty outshone even the most fashionable ladies. More than one gentleman eyed her with something other than polite interest. Aston wanted to plow his fist into their faces.

Mine. She's mine.

Except, Chasity wasn't now nor ever could be his.

Instead, Aston leveled each brazen bounder a glare meant to singe their eyelashes and shrivel their manhood. Only his friends and co-investors, the Earl of Clarendon and the Marquis of Sterling, were spared his murderous scowl.

Their stares were prompted by curiosity, naught else. Kingsley had the gall to wink before slipping an arm around his wife's waist and brushing a kiss above her ear.

Aston's regard caught on the ornate manicured garden. Several guests milled about outdoors. "The gardens. We should be able to find a spot to speak privately. I shall claim to be overheated or that you are joining your friends in admiring the roses."

In point of fact, it was likely hotter out of doors than in the drawing room.

"Slip your hand into the crook of my elbow and smile," he said beneath his breath.

Chasity complied, but the smile she fashioned was the practiced and professional upward sweep that held no genuine warmth or amusement.

Aston guided her toward the open French doors on the other side of the drawing room. Nodding and smiling at acquaintances, he wended them through the crowd at a brisk pace that discouraged others from engaging him in conversation.

A dark-haired middling-age woman glared daggers at Chasity. Another young woman who must've been her daughter, given their strong resemblance, peered at Aston as if he had sprouted another head.

There was no accounting for the oddities of *le beau monde*.

"I don't think this is a good idea," Chasity said in an urgent, hushed tone. "People will talk."

They would. They already were. It was what the *ton* did best.

Gossip. Speculate. Spread rumors.

Sliding her a sideways look, Aston gave her a crooked grin. "Don't you trust me?"

Her eyes grew round before she was forced to side-step an elderly dame wielding her cane like a saber as she bellowed to the two women in her company.

Aston and Chasity reached the threshold and stepped into the warm but refreshing air. The fragrance of roses and honeysuckle wafted past. Somewhere nearby, a fountain burbled happily.

"I do. Trust you that is, Aston."

Emotion blossomed behind Aston's chest, and he patted her hand resting in the crook of his elbow. "Excellent. I am honored, and I vow I'll never betray your confidence."

Shaking her head, she chuckled, a low husky rasp that took him by surprise.

"What's so entertaining?" God, how he loved her laugh. To see that joy twinkling in her eyes was an unexpected gift.

"You sound so earnest. So serious." She grinned in sincere amusement. "Like you were reciting a solemn oath."

It was on the tip of Aston's tongue to tell her that was precisely what he'd done, but a warning sounded somewhere in his brain.

Tread carefully. Don't make promises you cannot keep. Don't encourage trust or a reliance you cannot promise to fulfill.

Instead, he cast a judicious glance around the terrace and gardens. Chasity's friends milled about on the other side, admiring the admittedly stunning roses. A few people sent a distracted glance in his direction but just as swiftly turned their attention elsewhere.

Aston spotted the top of a small arbor hidden by a hedgerow and past a well-tended path. And blessedly shaded beneath trees. Perfect.

"Over there." He jutted his chin toward that portion of the garden.

They walked in silence, their shoes crunching on the gravel until they reached the arbor.

It was occupied.

A couple sat upon the bench, kissing. Well, more accurately, reclined and groped upon the bench.

Ah, another clandestine meeting. Except if one wanted to engage in a *tête-à-tête*, one ought to select a more discreet location.

Chasity slapped a gloved hand over her mouth, smothering a startled gasp. Her gaze shot to Aston's. And rather than shock, revulsion, or condemnation, hilarity sparkled in her eyes. Casting her attention to the footpath, Chasity turned her head away.

"Ahem." Aston loudly cleared his throat.

The man and woman jumped apart in a flurry of awkward elbows and legs.

At once, the gentleman scrambled to his feet and offered the scarlet-faced young woman his arm. They summoned stiff smiles and averted their gazes as they bustled past.

Chasity's shoulders shook with her suppressed laughter. Most women would've been scandalized, embarrassed, or curious. She, however, being Chasity, found the situation humorous.

"I'm sure they are hoping we don't say anything," Aston said with a wry grin.

She shrugged and looked behind her. "As I don't know either of them, I cannot think why I would. Besides, who am I to judge when...here *we* are." She made a sweeping gesture with her hand, indicating the small enclosure entwined with purple clematis.

"Ah, but we don't intend to engage in a forbidden kiss,"

Aston couldn't help but tease. He waggled his eyebrows. "Do we?"

She raised that winged blonde brow in the starchy manner that seemed to say, *enough of your foolishness,* and prompted immediate contriteness in her students.

Her primness merely goaded the devil on his shoulder. It amused Aston and made him want to tease her more. Chasity didn't laugh or smile enough. She might be excellent at teaching all manner of lessons, but Miss Chasity Noble didn't know how to live.

To relax and enjoy life. To have fun. *To love?*

"No, we shan't be kissing," she admonished with the prudishness of a seventy-year-old virgin nun.

Because that was who she really was or because that was who she'd been trained to be?

Aston had begun to suspect the Chasity Noble, assistant headmistress at Balderbrook's Institution for Genteel Ladies, was not the real Chasity Noble. That person had been stifled and subdued into submission by expectations and strictures.

Aston chuckled and indicated she should have a seat. "I was but jesting, Chasity."

"I know." She settled onto the bench and smoothed her skirts. A bird chirped above them, hidden somewhere in the tree's foliage. "Now, what is this mysterious plan you have concocted?"

Aston took the seat beside her. Their shoulders and thighs touched due to the bench's smallness. Lifting Chasity's hand, Aston kissed her knuckles.

Her pink mouth went soft at the corners, and her gaze grew tender. "What...are you doing?"

"The truth of it is, I've decided a kiss is a rather grand idea after all."

Her focus trailed to his mouth, and her tongue darted out for a fraction of a second.

"Why?" she whispered.

"Because I would regret it for the rest of my life if I did not kiss you." Aston leaned nearer until his mouth was a mere inch from hers.

"But only if you want to kiss me too, Chasity."

Her sweet breath, smelling of lemon and tea, fanned his cheek.

"I do, Aston. I really do."

Needing no further encouragement, Aston brushed his mouth across hers. A feather's touch. A wisp and no more. Once. Twice. Then he pressed fully into the tempting, velvety softness.

She sighed and snuggled closer, one hand coming to cup the back of his neck.

He shuddered from the intense sweetness and the all-engulfing emotion that squeezed his chest. Running his tongue along the seam of Chasity's lips, he encouraged her to open to him.

She hesitantly moved her mouth beneath his in acquiescence as she melted into his embrace.

Heaven. Surely this was heaven.

Oh, God, Aston silently prayed. *If only there was a way that she could be mine.*

Impossible, his realistic self reprimanded. *Grandfather would destroy her. Just as he did your parents.*

Then by all that was holy, Aston would savor this precious interlude. Cherish each murmur and sigh. The way her form fit perfectly against his and the magical way the world faded away until there was only Chasity and him. Sharing a forbidden kiss in a world that was impossibly unfair. For if life was fair and just, he would be able to give her his heart and love her until the end of his days.

The bird trilled again, and Chasity stiffened, then pulled away. Fingertips to her mouth, she gazed at him. Indigo eyes bright with surprise, pleasure, and, yes, desire, she stared.

"I'm sorry, Aston. We cannot. I cannot be compromised." She tried to smile but failed. "It would give Mrs. Crenshaw the weapon she needs to dismiss me."

She was right.

Aston should never have brought her out here. He was a selfish cad.

He drew a finger over her smooth-as-a-peach cheek. "I know, sweetheart. I know I should say I'm sorry, but I cannot regret kissing you. I've wanted to since I danced with you."

This time a nascent smile full of regret did bend her mouth upward. "Some things are just not meant to be, Aston." She put her hand over his heart. "*We* are not meant to be."

And he couldn't contradict her. She spoke what they both knew to be the truth.

"I'm sorry, Chasity. I wish it were otherwise with all of my being."

"There you are." Kellinggrave strode toward him, scarcely giving Chasity a glance. "An urgent missive has arrived for you from your grandfather."

How had grandfather known where Aston was?

Was he having Aston followed?

Likely, the interfering tosspot.

"Thank you." Aston broke the wax and scanned the short letter.

His dying uncle asked for him. How could he refuse? He couldn't, of course. Conley was as much a victim as Aston had been, only he'd found his escape in spirits.

Folding the rectangle, Aston stood. "I have to leave at once. We'll speak tomorrow at Balderbrook's Institution for Genteel Ladies, Chasity. I shall arrive early so we might finish our discussion."

"That will be fine." Nodding, she rose as well. "I hope nothing is amiss."

A rueful smile strained his lips. "With my family, something is always amiss." He glanced to Kellinggrave, who had retreated a respectful distance. "Might I trouble you for a ride to Berkeley Square?"

"Of course." He slid Chasity an indecipherable glance. Kellinggrave was a man of discretion. He'd not say a word about finding Chasity alone with Aston. "I shall have my phaeton brought 'round."

He strode away.

Chasity hoped Faith knew what she was getting herself into. From what Chasity had observed thus far, Kellinggrave had the personality of a rock.

Aston scraped a hand through his hair. "Chasity, about our kiss..."

She held up a hand.

"I think it best if we pretend it never happened, Aston. Call it a foolish whimsy. But neither of us is a fool." She stepped away, but before she left, she half-turned. "Perhaps it is best that we part ways. Before we become the very fools we spurn."

TWELVE

Darling of my heart. Your silence eviscerates me. Why don't you answer my letters? My heart grows heavier every day, and my soul is troubled. Have your parents punished you for eloping with me? Are they keeping my letters from you? I told you that you should go to live with my family in Cornwall until I could make arrangements for you to join me in Sweden. I know they would've welcomed you. I am going to write my brother and ask him to call upon you. I cannot sleep for worrying about you, my love.

~ Rt. Hon. Martin Oxley-Norton, Envoy to
Sweden in a letter to his wife, Audrey
Sent but intercepted by the
Duke of Monteagle - Audrey's father

Balderbrook's Institution for Genteel Ladies
Mrs. Crenshaw's office
24 August 1818

Aston hadn't come.

He wasn't here, and Chasity had been called before the board members and Mrs. Crenshaw. Given the censorious frowns and turned down mouths of the visitors, this was not a cordial meeting.

What had Mrs. Crenshaw told them?

Lies naturally, but what precisely?

Sitting tall in the unforgiving chair, Chasity slid a glance to Lady Balderbrook. The woman returned her regard with icy disdain. There would be no help from that quarter—no private audience to explain her suspicions.

Despair tried to raise its ugly little head, but Chasity quashed it with the same vehemence as she would have a nasty insect. If nothing else, her conscience was clear. She'd done nothing unethical, and God knew that to be the truth.

Mrs. Crenshaw couldn't say the same. She might get away with her duplicity now, but one day, she'd stand before the Lord and be held accountable. Unfortunately, that brought little comfort at this moment.

The clock chimed the half hour, and Chasity curled her toes into the soles of her shoes. This summons did not bode well. Not at all. The knot in her stomach coiled tighter and tighter until she felt physically ill.

Lady Jane Balderbrook, Mr. Theobald Bramblefink, and Mr. Pharris Potterburger had arrived seven minutes before ten of the clock. It was now half-past eleven. What had transpired during the hour and a half they'd been sequestered in Mrs. Crenshaw's office?

Where is Aston? her heart and soul cried.

When Josie had come to tell Chasity she was wanted in Mrs. Crenshaw's office and with instructions for her students to be given the morning off, Chasity had presumed Aston had arrived, and she hadn't noticed because she'd been in class.

Josie had accompanied Chasity down the corridor and

before they reached the headmistress's office, had pulled her into a salon reserved for guests.

Worried Mrs. Crenshaw would be irritated at her delay, Chasity had frowned. "Is something amiss, Josie?"

"I heard what you said to Mr. Terramier about Mrs. Crenshaw altering the books, Miss Noble." She thrust out her round chin and squared her sturdy shoulders. "I believe you. You wouldn't make something like that up."

The maid had already avowed to having her tongue cut out. Her continued loyalty touched Chasity.

"Thank you, Josie. Your confidence in me is appreciated." Chasity laid her hand upon the maid's arm. "If you're interested, a dear friend of mine has an opening for a maid. I told her about you. They are a well-to-do family but the nicest people. I'm not positive what the nature of your duties would be, but—"

"Yes! Oh, yes, Miss." Josie grabbed Chasity's hand between both of hers. "I'm ever so grateful. My days here are numbered. I know they are. I cannot seem to keep my mug shut, and the headmistress doesn't like me." Her brilliant smile faded, and worry crinkled her forehead. "Your friend won't mind my forwardness, will she?"

"No, I think she'll rather admire it. I'll give you her contact information and a letter of introduction before the day is over."

Josie grinned. "I shan't even give that hobgoblin notice."

Chasity hadn't needed to ask who the hobgoblin was.

At this very moment, Mrs. Crenshaw stood a few feet away. The headmistress appeared too smug and self-satisfied by far. A feline smile tipped her mouth up at the corners like a cat who'd just consumed a bowl of fresh cream. Or an innocent baby bird or squirrel.

"Do you know why we have summoned you, Miss

Noble?" Mr. Potterburger asked in a haughty yet emotionless tenor.

Slanting her head, Chasity examined him. Condemnation glittered in his judgmental gaze. "I do not."

I have a strong suspicion, however.

Mrs. Crenshaw must've convinced the board and benefactors that she'd done something worth being dismissed over. But what? And Aston hadn't come to implement his plan to save Chasity's position. His scheme mightn't have worked in any event. What had the missive contained that prompted him to leave yesterday afternoon suddenly?

Was that the reason he'd not arrived?

Couldn't he have sent a note around at least, explaining? So she wouldn't have waited for him? Wouldn't have placed her hope in his fanciful machinations, whatever they might've been? *Oh, God.* Panic welled within her in undulating waves, and bile burned the back of her throat.

Chasity forced herself to remain composed—at least outwardly. She needed her wits about her for whatever *this* was.

Writing the letters to the board and benefactors late last night had been a colossal waste of time. There was no need to post them now.

"Allow me to elucidate." Lady Balderbrook struck a dramatic pose. Her ladyship missed no opportunity to garner more attention even if her audience consisted of only four people.

"Mr. Bramblefink has detected several discrepancies in the accounting books." She swept her critical gaze over Chasity and then veered her attention to Mrs. Crenshaw. "We are given to understand that you keep the accounts?"

Chasity speared Mrs. Crenshaw a look meant to pin her to the wall.

Something dark and sinister glinted in the headmistress's gaze. She'd planned this all along. She'd set Chasity up to take the fall for her, and Chasity had blindly walked straight into the snare.

"At Mrs. Crenshaw's behest, I do *partially* keep the academy's bookkeeping ledgers updated," Chasity said.

She made sure to emphasize the partially bit.

"Mrs. Crenshaw always reviews the ledgers after I've recorded the entries, and I provide her with a list of any inconsistencies I have found. Invariably, there would be several that I couldn't account for."

Mr. Potterburger drew his grizzled eyebrows together over the bridge of the most spectacularly bulbous nose—rather like an elephant seal she'd seen a drawing of in a book once. The furry things above his eyes seemed to have a life of their own, writhing and wriggling like ugly, gray caterpillars.

"Are you suggesting Mrs. Crenshaw has...that she...?" he stumbled about for the right words. "That is, that *she* has made inaccurate entries?"

Chasity folded her hands and gripped them together so tightly that her fingertips grew numb.

In for a penny, in for a pound.

"Yes. There are entries in Mrs. Crenshaw's hand without a receipt or a bill. Often, a figure I recorded was altered without any documentation as to why it was changed. Mrs. Crenshaw recorded expenditures for goods and services that to my knowledge never were provided or delivered."

Chasity drew in a steadying breath, feeling the hatred boring from Mrs. Crenshaw's hostile gaze as surely as if she'd stabbed Chasity.

"When I questioned the expenses, Mrs. Crenshaw always had an excuse and promised to give me the documentation. Yet in the two months that I have been partly keeping the ledgers, I have not been provided a single validation for those funds."

There. Chasity had said it. Laid the accusation bare. She'd all but called Mrs. Crenshaw an embezzler and a thief.

Studying their judgmental expressions, one after the other, Chasity detected no sympathy, no remorse, and most importantly and dishearteningly, no hint that they believed she spoke the truth. These people had already made up their minds. She could see it in the unyielding angles of their faces and in the condemnation in their hardened gazes.

"How convenient that you allege Mrs. Crenshaw guilty of the very crimes she has accused you of." Mr. Bramblefink adjusted his monocle and took Chasity's measure. "It is a good thing we arrived for the inspection a month early, or you might've had time to conceal your thievery. 'Tis an excellent thing indeed that Mrs. Crenshaw reviewed the books yesterday and discovered your subterfuge."

"I am no thief, Mr. Bramblefink, and I resent your implication," Chasity said. She speared Mrs. Crenshaw an accusatory glance. "*I* am not the person who modified the entries. At all times, I have conducted myself with integrity and honesty."

Mrs. Crenshaw made a rude noise, nearly a snort of contempt, while Mr. Potterburger harrumphed his disapproval.

Chasity slowly rose. Once upright, she stiffened her spine and steeled her jaw. "I suggest you examine Mr. Aston Terramier's personnel file. He is the dance master and music instructor. Mrs. Crenshaw drafted a private contract and is paying him ten pounds a month. Should she terminate him, she owes him the full year's wages."

Erring on the side of prudence, Chasity opted not to share

Viscount Woolbury's blackmailing Mrs. Crenshaw or the headmistress's infatuation with Aston.

"*Ten* pounds?" Lady Balderbrook gasped and fluttered a hand around her scrawny throat. "That's outrageous."

"I say. That is excessive, and whyever would you include a clause to pay the man all of his wages if he was terminated?" A finger to his cheek, Mr. Potterburger leveled Mrs. Crenshaw a shrewd glance. "I should like to see Mr. Terramier's employment file, if you please."

"Of course, Mr. Potterburger. I don't know what Miss Noble is referring to." Mrs. Crenshaw sat at her desk and, after pulling a key on a chain from around her neck, unlocked one of the drawers. "Miss Noble is merely desperate to paint me the villain and has concocted a wholly unbelievable tale to do so."

Because you are the villain.

Chasity clenched her jaw to keep from saying as much.

Mrs. Crenshaw shuffled around in the desk drawer. "Ah, here we are."

She withdrew the folder and placed it on her desk. Shoving it across the top, she slid Chasity a triumphant look.

In a heartbeat, Chasity understood.

The witch had removed and likely destroyed the contract. This was the file Chasity had seen on the headmistress's desk. The one Mrs. Crenshaw had slid beneath the ledgers.

"You'll find Mr. Terramier's letter of resignation, which I received yesterday afternoon, in the file as well." Mrs. Crenshaw fairly crowed in triumph.

"His...resignation?" Chasity choked down the rest of the words ready to spill off her tongue.

Aston had already resigned?

What was it he'd said yesterday at tea?

She searched her memory.

I've decided to resign next month from my position at Balderbrook's Institution for Genteel Ladies.

He hadn't said he'd already given notice, but Aston also didn't say he hadn't. She'd assumed he hadn't yet.

"Yes, his letter of resignation," Mrs. Crenshaw reaffirmed with an insincere smile.

"I have it here," Mr. Potterburger said to no one in particular, waving the foolscap for all to see. "Terramier. Terramier. Why do I know that name?"

"Because, Mr. Potterburger, Mr. Terramier is Viscount Woolbury's rapscallion grandson," Lady Balderbrook provided with the air of one who is superior in all things. "The boy flaunts his grandfather's wishes and his birthright and carries on like common riffraff."

Mrs. Crenshaw laid her palms flat on her desk and rose, leaning forward.

"And if I didn't already have grounds for dismissing you, Miss Noble, your inappropriate relationship with Mr. Terramier was confirmed at the Trentholms' tea yesterday."

Looking entirely too self-satisfied, she fussed with the lace at the collar of her gown.

"My what?"

Confirmed? By who?

"Lady Finch-Hatten observed you disappearing into a remote part of the garden with Mr. Terramier. She is Esmerelda Finch-Hatten's mother and saw fit to pen me a note yesterday afternoon informing me of your scandalous conduct. She thought it unfitting behavior for an assistant headmistress to dally with a gentleman."

Chasity well knew who Lady Finch-Hatten was, and now she understood the visual daggers the woman had speared her all afternoon yesterday.

"Isn't my Esmerelda the most graceful of dancers?

"My Esmerelda plays the violin like an angel.

"Esmerelda cannot share a chamber. She is such a light sleeper. She must? Well, then naturally, she must have her choice of beds. What do you mean she cannot breakfast in her chamber? Esmerelda's toast mustn't have any crust on it."

And on and on and on.

Her elder daughter, Miss Saphira Finch-Hatten, had attended a prestigious finishing school in Paris, and thus, Balderbrook's Institution for Genteel Ladies had been spared the busybody's interference before now.

Lady Finch-Hatten routinely remarked on the inferiority of Balderbrook's compared to *L'Académie Pour la Bienséance et le Decorum.* What a shame she hadn't enrolled her younger daughter in the French seminary as well.

The woman was no pebble in one's shoe. She was a monstrous, annoying boulder.

Chasity drew in a shaky breath. Everything was falling apart. "My friends were in the garden as well, and taking the air with Mr. Terramier is hardly scandalous or a dalliance."

That kiss was, but no one had seen it.

Nausea roiled in her stomach.

Had they?

No, she was sure of it.

This was nothing more than a jealous woman's revenge.

If Mrs. Crenshaw couldn't have Aston, she'd make sure Chasity couldn't either and that her reputation was destroyed to boot. Chasity had been right all along. Those speculative covert glances Mrs. Crenshaw had turned on her these past months were more than disapproving. There'd been malice and calculation disguised in the depths too.

Mr. Bramblefink and Mr. Potterburger finished examining Aston's employment folder.

"I see nothing out of the ordinary," Mr. Bramblefink said.

"There isn't a contract with the terms you have suggested, Miss Noble."

Lady Balderbrook sniffed disdainfully. "I think it is clear to us all what must be done. I had such high hopes for you, Miss Noble. What a disappointment you've turned out to be. It all comes down to breeding in the end, doesn't it? You simply cannot make a silk purse out of a sow's ear, even if the sow is a pretty sow with pretty manners."

Had she really just compared Chasity to a pig? A pretty pig?

Lady Balderbrook turned her back and walked to the window, where she idly fingered the fringe on her reticule.

"Miss Noble, you are dismissed without reference," Mr. Potterburger said in the same tone one shooed a stray dog from a bakery.

Though she had expected it, Chasity winced as if struck.

Why did the wicked always prevail?

For the life of her, she could not call forth an appropriate scripture to seize onto for strength and comfort as she normally did when distraught. Anger such as she'd never known sluiced through her veins at the injustice, and she fisted her hands lest she slap the smirk off of Mrs. Crenshaw's face.

God help me, I know it's wrong, but I despise her.

She'd ask for forgiveness later when her anger had cooled and common sense had returned—in a month or six.

Unable to keep the victory from her tone, Mrs. Crenshaw pointed to the door. "Pack your belongings and depart Balderbrook's Institution for Genteel Ladies within the hour."

"I am owed wages." Chasity would need every cent until she procured new employment. She had her small savings, but the funds wouldn't last long after paying for lodgings, fuel, and other necessities. Even if she economized, six months was all the longer she could survive without income.

For she'd already decided she couldn't return to Haven House and Academy for the Enrichment of Young Women. Mercy had left for the country this morning, and Chasity had no idea where Joy was staying in London. Besides, she had too much pride to impose upon either newlywed.

"What audacity!" Lady Balderbrook spun to face her, fairly vibrating in righteous outrage. "Consider your wages partial payment for the funds you cannot account for, and consider yourself fortunate that we don't bring charges against you. I would personally see to it that you never worked in London again, but I shall not besmirch Balderbrook's Institution for Genteel Ladies with such ignominy. Leave before I change my mind and have you arrested!"

In a daze, her mind reeling, Chasity turned toward the door.

Staying and fighting would prove useless. Her only thought at this moment was to escape. In case her ladyship did change her mind and had her arrested.

God help me.

A sharp rap echoed at the door, but Aston shoved the panel open before the headmistress bid entry. He wore the same clothes he'd worn to tea, only now they were rumpled. Dark circles framed his coffee-brown eyes, and stubble shadowed his angular jaw. He looked like he hadn't slept.

"Chasity?" His attention veered to those behind her.

She forced her gaze to meet his. Great, hot tears pooled in her eyes, but she would not cry in front of these horrid, evil people, by all that was holy. They would not have that victory.

"You're too late," she managed on a strangled croak before fleeing the room.

THIRTEEN

After much prayer and consideration, I believe you should be aware that the Rt. Hon. Martin Oxley-Norton called last week. He's a British diplomat and claims to be your father. He says he only became aware of your existence because the Duke of Monteagle recently died. A journal was discovered, which also contained unopened letters from Mr. Oxley-Norton to Lady Audrey Blankenly. She was the Duke of Monteagle's eldest daughter, and according to Mr. Oxley-Norton, they were secretly wed before he was sent as an Envoy to Sweden. Naturally, I could not presume you would want to meet him or know if he is truly your father. However, Lady Audrey died in childbirth, and you were brought to Haven House and Academy for the Enrichment of Young Ladies shortly thereafter. Audrey means noble, and that is how I selected your surname, Chasity. I have enclosed Mr. Oxley-Norton's direction should you decide you wish to contact him. He has asked that you do so.

~ Mrs. Hester Shepherd, Proprietress,
in a letter to Miss Chasity Noble

Enroute to Balderbrook's
Institution for Genteel Ladies

Balderbrook's Institution for Genteel Ladies
Still in Mrs. Crenshaw's office
Fifteen very unpleasant minutes later

Aston had never laid hands on a woman with violent intent, but at this moment, his fingers itched to wrap around Rafaela Crenshaw's neck and shake her into unconsciousness. It had only taken him a few minutes of questioning to understand what the scheming harpy had done.

She'd convinced the board and benefactors that Chasity was the culprit and not herself. Except, he had witnesses to Chasity's confession last week, and he had a copy of his contract that proved the headmistress had overstepped her authority.

More fool him, he ought to have questioned her when she hired him. He hadn't been flattered by her generosity but had honestly believed the school had generous patrons and, unlike most seminaries, chose to pay instructors well.

He should've known better.

Aston felt used, stupid, and like an utter arse.

He'd also let Chasity down by not being here when the benefactors arrived. That he couldn't have avoided. Uncle Conley passed quietly in his sleep at thirteen minutes past three this morning. It had taken Aston until almost eight to find his sot of a cousin passed out in a gaming hell.

Werner had chosen to drink himself into oblivion rather than be at his father's side when he died. After depositing his soused cousin at their grandfather's Berkeley Square house, Aston had been forced to endure an hour of complaints and a litany of condemnations from the viscount.

Jaw set, he squelched his harsh replies, reminding himself that Grandfather had just lost his only living son, and from Werner's pallor and weight loss, he might soon follow in his father's wake.

Which, God help him, meant Aston was the next in line to inherit.

Would Werner wed his lady in a few days as planned?

Strictures required him to mourn his father for a year. Regardless, knowing their mercenary grandfather, he'd insist the wedding take place. After all, an heir was more important than anything. Even honoring your son's death.

Both of Grandfather's sons had predeceased the rabid old tosspot. If he grieved at all, he hid it well.

Enough of that.

Filling his lungs with air, Aston clasped his hands behind his back and tipped back onto his heels.

"Mr. Terramier, it offends my sensibilities that you should arrive looking like you've slept in your clothes." Lady Balderbrook raised a superior nose. "We know what we need to know in any event. Fortunately, you have already tendered your resignation, or you would be dismissed along with Miss Noble."

Aston peeled his gaze from the haughty dame and stabbed Mrs. Crenshaw with an incredulous glance.

"My resignation? I haven't tendered my resignation as yet. In fact, given the circumstances, I am not the least inclined to do so. Particularly as the entire balance of my contract is due at once if I'm dismissed. And if you are dismissing me, I'll have the remaining two hundred and twenty pounds now."

Bramblefink's and Potterburger's jaws came unhinged. Bug-eyed, they gaped wide enough for a pelican to nest inside their mouths.

Mrs. Crenshaw swayed on her feet and grasped a chair for

support while Lady Balderbrook, for once, was rendered utterly speechless. Her mouth worked repeatedly, but nothing but strange croaks and squeaks came forth.

"What say you?" Theobald Bramblefink finally regained his senses and shoved his spectacles up his nose as he gave Mrs. Crenshaw a gimlet stare. "I saw the letter of resignation in your personnel folder myself, Mr. Terramier."

He gestured to the open file atop the headmistress's desk.

Puffing out his barrel chest, Pharris Potterburger grabbed his lapels. "What manner of balderdashery is this?" He swung his accusing gaze between Aston and Mrs. Crenshaw, then pointed to the folder. "I also read your contract, Mr. Terramier. There is no outlandish mention of such a clause. Two hundred and twenty pounds. What rubbish."

"Indeed," Mrs. Crenshaw offered weakly, still clutching the chair with a white-knuckled grip.

Aston would vow that was the only reason she still remained on her feet.

The game was up, and she realized it. What was more, she had grossly underestimated Aston's response for what she'd so cruelly done to Chasity. Not a jot of mercy or compassion would she see from him. In this, he was his grandfather's spawn after all.

Potterburger chuckled a dry, hacking cackle. "Why, one would have to be demented to include such a provision."

Aye, demented might be exactly what Rafaela Crenshaw was. Perhaps Bedlam would serve as well as Newgate.

Aston reached inside his coat and removed his copy of the contract. "Please, read my employment agreement for yourselves. I assure you, it is authentic, and if you compare my signature on this document to the one that is supposedly on my resignation and the other contract in my folder, I'm positive you'll find they are not the same."

Mrs. Crenshaw made a strangled sound and clutched at her throat before pointing a shaky finger at him. "He's conspiring with that trollop to ruin me. I knew they were plotting something nefarious, but you see how far they have gone?"

She'd turned a sickly shade somewhere between spoiled cream and rancid porridge.

Lady Balderbrook narrowed her eyes and studied Aston for a long moment. "You're very much like your father, young Terramier. He was a man of strong principles too. I cannot say I always agreed with him, but he stood his ground when he believed in something."

She held out a black kid-gloved hand. "Let me see."

Aston passed the papers over, which she quickly perused. As she read, her mouth pinched impossibly tighter and tighter.

"Well," she said as she handed the document to Mr. Potterburger for his examination. "I believe I understand exactly what has transpired here."

Before she could explain, a hesitant knock caught the attention of the room's occupants.

"What now?" Mrs. Crenshaw grumbled, but she didn't bid anyone enter.

Mr. Bramblefink raised his eyebrows as he wiped his monocle with a handkerchief. "Aren't you going to answer, Mrs. Crenshaw?"

"Oh, very well." She sank unsteadily into the chair behind her desk. She really didn't look at all well. Good. It was justice for what she'd put Chasity through.

"Come in," she bid rather hoarsely.

Mrs. Ramsbottom entered, followed by the saucy maid.

What was her name?

Ah, yes. Josie.

"You asked to see us, Mr. Terramier?" Mrs. Ramsbottom studiously avoided looking directly at Mrs. Crenshaw.

Aston summoned an encouraging smile. Dead tired, his eyes gritty, and feeling like he'd been run over by a buggy, he raked a hand through his hair.

"Mrs. Ramsbottom, would you kindly tell everyone what you told me earlier today?"

She swallowed audibly and twisted her hands together. Her gaze darted about the room like a caged bird.

Astonishingly, Lady Balderbrook's features softened. "Do go on, Mrs. Ramsbottom. You needn't fear retribution. I give you my word."

She gave Mrs. Crenshaw a quelling glower. The headmistress wilted farther into her chair, but sullen anger glittered in her unrepentant gaze.

"I...I heard Miss Noble telling Mr. Terramier that she feared something dishonest was going on with the account books. She was so upset that she was weeping. Miss Noble thought perhaps she should contact the board and benefactors with her suspicions."

"She's lying," Mrs. Crenshaw screeched. "That fat cow has always been jealous of my position and Miss Noble's too."

"Silence!" Lady Balderbrook thundered, causing Mr. Bramblefink to jump and Mr. Potterburger to drop his spectacles.

"She's telling the truth." Josie edged around the plump instructor and bobbed an unnecessary curtsy. "Begging your pardon, but I heard Miss Noble too. I was standing in the corridor behind Mrs. Ramsbottom and heard every word. Miss Noble was most distraught that something wasn't right with the books. She was also concerned about how that would impact the school, the staff, and the students."

The headmistress lurched to her feet. She threw her arms

out to her sides. "This is utterly ridiculous. You would take the word of a servant and a teacher over the school's director?"

"Not just a servant and an instructor, but also the assistant headmistress and myself." Aston jabbed his thumb at his chest. "I could have you arrested for forging my name on that resignation and contract."

"I do believe you have a great deal of explaining to do, Mrs. Crenshaw," Mr. Bramblefink said. "Just where are the accounting ledgers? I should like to examine them at this time."

"No! That is...wait." Mrs. Crenshaw summoned a sickly smile. "Are you forgetting Lady Finch-Hatten felt compelled to write and tell me she witnessed Mr. Terramier and Miss Noble in the gardens at the Marquess of Trenholm's yesterday?"

That must've been the woman glaring at Chasity and who'd eavesdropped when Aston explained to his hostess why he'd been called away. And she'd taken it upon herself to blacken Chasity's character to Mrs. Crenshaw, giving the vile woman more fodder to use against Chasity.

"I presume Lady Finch-Hatten also told you I'd been summoned to my grandfather's because my uncle was dying?"

Was her ladyship worried Aston was courting Chasity and that the marriage she and her husband had arranged between Saphira and Aston with Grandfather wouldn't be honored? Because it assuredly wouldn't be. The woman would be a horror of a mother-in-law.

He grimaced and swept his hand down his front. "That is why I am disheveled and why I must beg your pardon for my appearance and tardiness. My uncle died early this morning."

Everyone in the office looked appropriately sympathetic and murmured polite condolences except the headmistress. She clamped her lips tighter than a beggar's purse.

"And you presumed I wouldn't come today and gambled that no one would know that you forged my resignation." Aston tapped his chin. "I believe that's fraud. It seems to me you've committed multiple crimes, Mrs. Crenshaw."

He angled toward Josie. "Would you send a groom to request the magistrate make haste here?"

Casting Mrs. Crenshaw a triumphant glance, Josie nodded and grinned. "At once, sir."

She all but ran from the chamber.

Lady Balderbrook sailed to the middle of the office. She said nothing for several *tick-tocks* of the clock. "Mrs. Ramsbottom, is it?"

Mrs. Ramsbottom turned chalk-white, but she nodded. "Yes, your ladyship."

"You are appointed the temporary director of this branch of Balderbrook's Institution for Genteel Ladies. Mrs. Crenshaw is relieved of her duties."

The headmistress gasped and then, with a withering glare, made to storm from the room.

Oh, no, you don't. You shan't escape that easily.

She'd be in the coach and headed into obscurity in ten minutes with the stash of money she'd pilfered from the school tucked in her valise, he'd be bound.

Arms folded, Aston stepped into her path. "You'll not leave my sight until the magistrate has taken you into custody."

Mr. Bramblefink took Mrs. Crenshaw by the elbow. "I believe you should wait for the magistrate over here."

She didn't protest as he led her away. Perhaps she'd finally realized there was no escape for her crimes. He led her to a chair positioned in a corner the farthest from the door and then took up a sentinel's post beside her. Mr. Potterburger joined him, and the men exchanged knowing glances.

They didn't trust the headmistress anymore than Aston did. Which was no farther than he could hurl a coach and four. In other words, not at all.

Several minutes passed as Mrs. Ramsbottom and Lady Balderbrook discussed the sudden change in the school's administration.

Aston was bone tired. All he wanted to do was to crawl into bed and sleep until tomorrow. No, what he really yearned to do was to find his lovely Chasity, take her into his arms, apologize for being late, and assure her things would work out. Somehow, he'd ensure they did.

In Italy?

That trip might have to be postponed. There'd been no firm date of departure in any event. The truth of it was, Aston had used the business trip to Italy as an escape. He couldn't stay on at Balderbrook's and cost Chasity her position, and he couldn't do what he desired most either.

Make her his wife.

And have her treated as horridly as his mother had been? To be called a whore? To be treated worse than the lowest slattern?

Aston had stormed from the viscount's that day after he'd called his mother a slut for the last time. He'd not continue to live where such a vile man disparaged Aston's mother simply because she'd didn't possess the requisite blue blood.

Lady Balderbrook's crisp tones ended his reverie, and he smothered a yawn behind his hand.

"The task will not be easy, Mrs. Ramsbottom, as you will be short of staff for the time being, and, most likely, an investigation will occur." Lady Balderbrook drew herself up in the regal way women of position had perfected and actually fashioned a benevolent smile. "If you are up to the task, I believe a woman of your integrity would do well."

"Oh, yes, my lady." Joy blossomed across Mrs. Ramsbottom's face like a flower opening to the sun. "I should be honored."

"What about Miss Noble's position?" Aston inquired.

Would she even want to stay after this debacle?

"Unfortunately, until the investigation is complete and a decision has been rendered about the actual embezzler, Miss Noble cannot be reinstated." Mr. Potterburger eyed the stone-faced Mrs. Crenshaw distastefully. "However, once the issue has been resolved, I see no reason, if found innocent, that Miss Noble cannot resume her duties."

He looked to Mr. Bramblefink, who muttered, "Excellent," and then to Lady Balderbrook.

She inclined her head. "Just so."

Aston cursed inwardly. He'd not saved Chasity's position as he'd intended. At least not for the short term. He needed to speak with her at once. She must be beside herself.

"I beg your pardon, but I must be away. My address is in my employment folder, and the magistrate can reach me there for my statement. My contract, please." He extended his hand, and Mr. Bramblefink obligingly handed him the document.

After folding the papers, Aston returned them to a pocket inside his jacket.

He'd have to be addled to leave such an important piece of evidence where it might *accidentally* get misplaced or destroyed as Mrs. Crenshaw's copy had.

Over the next few days, Aston would be busy with Uncle Conley's funeral arrangements. He'd agreed to take on the task because his uncle had asked him to. Odd that he hadn't asked his son, but perhaps he believed Werner would be too over-wrought. Or, in truth, wholly inept.

And then there was the reading of Conley's will. Aston had hoped to avoid that tediousness, but Uncle Conley had explicitly asked him to be present at the reading. On second thought, the magistrate might need to call at Grandfather's home. "Or the magistrate can find me at Sutton House, Berkeley Square."

After giving a brief bow, Aston left the office and hurried down the corridor. He had no idea where Chasity's bedchamber was, but he'd wager all of the sleeping areas were on the upper story.

Josie came hustling down the passageway, breathless and her cheeks flushed. "I'm sorry I didn't return sooner, but... ah...Cook needed my help in the kitchen."

She wiped her hands across her wet cheeks and forced a bright smile. It didn't reach her red-rimmed eyes.

Had she received a scolding?

"I've sent the groom for the magistrate as you asked, Mr. Terramier. He left about twenty minutes ago."

"Well done, Josie." Already halfway up the risers, Aston paused. "Where is Miss Noble's chamber?"

Josie blinked against the tears swimming in her eyes once more. She shook her head and swallowed hard.

"She's...she's gone, sir." Tears streamed down her face. "She left with a groom."

FOURTEEN

I don't believe I have ever met a more infuriating or perplexing man in my life. Lord Kellinggrave admitted he recognized me at the Trentholms' tea. When I asked him why he ignored me, he said he never mixes business with pleasure. That's not the entire tale, however. I have discovered his lordship only hired me after losing a wager. My employment is the result. I shall explain the details the next time I see you. Nevertheless, suffice it to say, his lordship doesn't believe I can perform an amanuensis's duties. He expects me to quit and is doing his utmost to push me to the brink. I mean to prove the rogue wrong on all accounts. Pray for me, because as you well know, I struggle to bridle my tongue, and patience isn't a virtue I possess. I may box his ears before all is said and done.

~ Miss Faith Roth in a hastily written
note to Miss Purity Mayfield

A dusty road to London
24 August 1818

I shall not cry. I shall not cry. I. Shall. Not. Cry.

Thank goodness Chasity's unadorned gray bonnet shielded her face from Gibney's curious glances, else the groom might see her struggling for control. Jaw aching from clenching her teeth against the tears surging in the back of her throat, Chasity stared straight ahead. She saw nothing except beloved Aston's face, etched with fatigue and regret as she'd fled Mrs. Crenshaw's office.

Each bounce of the wagon jarred her bones and slammed her bum relentlessly on the unpadded bench, cruelly reminding Chasity of her sudden reverse in fortunes. She'd gone from assistant headmistress in a prestigious academy to a criminal accused of theft and immorality. From safety and security to an unknown future fraught with uncertainty and possible peril.

A wave of dread sent a cold chill along her spine despite the day's heat. Her two biggest fears, hardship and instability, had come to pass.

How had everything gone to Hades in a chamber pot so dashed quickly?

It hadn't taken Chasity long to pack her possessions in her two valises. She'd left Balderbrook's Institution for Genteel Ladies without telling anyone but Josie goodbye. The dear maid had sobbed and promised to present her letter of introduction at the Trentholms' household that very day. She'd also had a few choice words about Mrs. Crenshaw's questionable parentage and a reference to the woman's face resembling an old gander's hind end.

Chasity was too hurt and humiliated to seek out anyone else to say farewell. In any event, Aston had still been sequestered in the headmistress's office. Like an injured animal, she only wanted to escape and hide somewhere, nursing her wounds until she recovered.

She would recover.

She wasn't so melodramatic as to believe otherwise. But it would take time—perhaps a great deal of time—and she would never be the same. Outwardly, she might appear healthy and whole, but inside, a terrible scar would remain.

Placing her trust in anyone from this point forward would not come easily either.

Aston's betrayal stung the worst. Like a rusty blade plunged into her stomach and twisted over and over. The agony was so visceral, she pressed a palm to her belly. Except if she were entirely fair, she couldn't even honestly call his actions a betrayal.

He'd merely told her he was resigning so that he could go to Italy.

Italy. So far, far away.

For how long?

Did it matter?

No. No, it did not. Not now.

A vice squeezed her heart, and an agonized sob lodged in her throat.

Tears burning behind her eyelids, Chasity forced herself to acknowledge she'd probably never see Aston again. Out of everything involved in this impossible tangle, that fact was the most painful. She hadn't been able to bid him goodbye and Godspeed. To wish him success and a happy life.

She'd never look into those warm brown eyes and see his cocky grin. Enjoy the pleasure of seeing his masculine grace as he danced or listen to the lyrical tenor of his deep voice.

Was there any detail about Aston that hadn't been carved into her memory?

Into her heart? Her very soul?

Even though she'd known nothing could come of her growing fascination with him, and their situation was impossible, she'd foolishly let Aston creep into her heart. Oh, it hadn't been intentional. In fact, she fought her feelings with logic and reason and all manner of persuasive arguments.

In the end, all of her efforts to remain impassive and unaffected had all been for naught.

For it seemed the heart would have what the heart would have. Mayhap that was why so many scriptures cautioned one to guard one's heart. No, those texts usually pertained to evil, not to love—to loving someone.

Love was the most glorious thing ever created. The sentiment changed one. Shaped and molded a person into someone they hardly recognized at times. A person who would willingly sacrifice anything and everything if they were loved so intensely in return.

Perchance that was the way it was with some women. They wanted what they couldn't have, and although the situation was hopeless, an irrational, foolish, gullible part of them still believed their love could conquer all. Mrs. Crenshaw was a perfect example of unrequited love, and look what her disappointment had caused her to do.

Except...that premise wasn't entirely true.

A deficit in Mrs. Crenshaw's character brought about her wicked decisions and schemes. Or a complete lack of morality and decency. Many people endured unreciprocated love and didn't turn into corrupt criminals, willing to send an innocent person to prison to pay for the crimes the vile bounder had committed.

Swallowing the bitter lump of grief in her throat, Chasity touched a bent knuckle to the corner of her eye to catch an escaping droplet. The inside of her cheek would be chewed to ribbons before they reached London, and the school was a mere two miles outside the city.

Thank the Lord she'd been able to catch a ride into

London with Gibney. He'd been sent to town for supplies and had gladly taken her aboard the wagon when she'd requested a ride. It would save her a good while walking and reserve her energy to find a place to stay tonight.

"It's sorry I be to see ye leave the school, Miss Noble." Gibney gave her a side-eyed look. He wouldn't ask why she was leaving, but curiosity danced in his sympathetic blue eyes. "Ye were one of the kind ones. Ye and Mr. Terramier. Ye'll be missed, that's for sure."

"Thank you," Chasity whispered, certain he'd hear the heartbreak in her voice if she said anything more. Or that the tears she valiantly kept in check would spring forth, and she wouldn't be able to stop sobbing.

In the end, kindness and decency hadn't mattered. Honesty and integrity, faith and loyalty had been no match for wickedness and deceit.

"Where can I drop ye?" Gibney adjusted his position on the seat and flicked the reins as he glanced overhead. The trees lining this section of the road provided welcome shade from the heat of the late August day.

Where, indeed?

She had nowhere to go. Not with Mercy on her way to Kelvingrove Park.

"Do you know of a respectable lodging house?" she asked, trying to sound confident and nonchalant. Like such a query was a common thing. "Not too expensive, but clean and in a reputable part of town?"

Gibney gave her an odd look, his severe eyebrows diving together. "Yer not stayin' with a friend or relative?"

Of course, he'd assume that she would, and his innocent question reminded her just how precarious her situation had become.

Chasity shook her head.

"I haven't any family, and most of my friends don't live in London. Unfortunately, the only one that has a home here left for the country this morning."

Why she was explaining to Gibney, she couldn't imagine. A simple no would've sufficed.

Clucking his tongue in empathy, he nodded.

"Aye, I do know a decent place, Miss Noble. It's run by the mother of a friend of mine who died in the war. If she has room, she'll take ye in for me. I was with Dutton when he passed. I brought her his effects and shared his last words with her. He'd said she was the best mum a man could have. I like to think it brought her peace."

His voice had grown gravelly, and he made a rough sound before clearing his throat.

"War is hell," he muttered hoarsely.

"I'm sorry for your loss, Gibney."

What else did one say?

Though words could shred flesh from bone, they did little to comfort in a moment like this.

He raised a beefy shoulder and pulled his cap down farther onto his broad forehead.

"We'd best make haste then. I'm to pick up the weekly supplies instead of Bexon because he was sent to fetch the magistrate."

The magistrate? Oh, God.

Nodding his head sagely, he whistled. "Some unlucky bloke's facin' a stay at Newgate, I'd guess. The magistrate is only called to officiate the most serious cases."

Was that true?

Chasity's blood ran cold.

Was she to be arrested after all then?

Wouldn't they have kept her at Balderbrook's Institution for Genteel Ladies if that was the case? Unless Mrs. Crenshaw had contrived another dastardly lie of some sort. Something more dire than theft and embezzlement?

Fisting her hands, Chasity set her jaw. Oh, how she despised that villainous woman.

A shiver scuttled across Chasity's shoulders, and she couldn't prevent looking behind them as the wagon rumbled along. Except for the sun's rays filtering through the trees, the road remained empty as far as she could see in the distance. Still, the sooner they reached London, the sooner she'd be able to breathe with ease.

"Could we hurry, Gibney? I'm not feeling at all well."

"Aye, miss." He flicked the reins again, urging the docile team into a cantor. "Get on with ye," he urged the horses. Dust puffed up from the horses' hooves and blanketed them in a fine layer of grit.

Twenty minutes later, Gibney steered the wagon before a sturdy three-story house. The place needed a fresh coat of white paint but otherwise appeared tidy. A calico tabby sunned herself across the top stair and made no effort to move when Gibney knocked upon the cheery green door.

In a surprisingly short time, Chasity found herself installed in a small, stark chamber.

A rickety washstand with a corroded mirror, a basin and pitcher, a small towel, and a covered chamber pot on the bottom shelf stood in one corner. The other corner served as a makeshift wardrobe with several wooden pegs extending from the wall.

She'd been tempted to give a different name when the proprietress asked for hers, but that would make Gibney suspicious. In truth, Chasity was surprised the groom hadn't made the connection between her hasty departure from Balderbrook's Institution for Genteel Ladies the unexpected summons for a magistrate.

As kind as Gibney was, he wasn't altogether quick-witted. Mrs. Pottkotter said he'd received a head injury during the war, and the blow had left him a bit daft. Gentle and hard-working but not too terribly bright—that was Gibney.

If Mrs. Crenshaw and the others were set on arresting Chasity, she had no doubt Gibney would be interrogated. He'd have no choice but to reveal where he'd left her. This was but a reprieve.

She bit the inside of her cheek.

Mayhap she should spend the majority of her funds and, under an assumed name, buy fare on a mail coach.

To where?

How would she survive once she arrived at this unknown destination?

"Rent is due every Saturday."

The proprietress's no-nonsense tone brought Chasity back to the present. She'd have to logically explore her options tonight and make a decision. Morning was soon enough to put whatever plan she settled on into action. At least she hoped she had until morning and no lawman would come banging upon the door in the dead of night.

"All meals are taken in the dining room—no exceptions. There's a bathing room down the hall. Forth door on the right. Baths are a guinea and need to be scheduled in advance to make sure there's hot water enough."

At least there was that. Chasity had worried the washstand was her only option for bathing. But did she dare spare a guinea once a week to wash her hair?

Would she be here a week?

Never before had Chasity been so conflicted and confused. So unsure of herself and what her future held. What path to set her feet upon. Did she stay and risk arrest? No court would take her word over Lady Balderbrook's, of that, she was positive.

Despair washed over her in unrelenting waves.

Unfair, her soul cried.

The landlady eyed Chasity up and down. "I run a respectable establishment, Miss Noble. No men callers in your chamber. Ever. Or you'll be out in two shakes of a lamb's tail."

"Of course," Chasity said, glancing around. "I don't know any men."

Save for Aston.

The furnishings were worn and dated, but the place was well-scrubbed, and there wasn't any sign of vermin. Not even a cobweb in a forgotten corner collecting dust.

In addition to a narrow bed with a nightstand on one side and a bureau on the other, a small settee had been situated at the end of the bed. It faced an unlit hearth, bracketed by a mantle with two shelves made of indeterminable wood.

The scarred wooden floor was bare, but a pair of what might've once been green curtains covered the two windows. Though it could never be called cozy, all in all, it wasn't a horrible place.

"Thank you for letting me a room." Chasity untied and removed her bonnet. "I'm very grateful."

"*Hmph.* See that you don't make me regret it." The landlady planted her hands on her wide hips and nodded in satisfaction. "Dinner is at seven. I'll send up Tildy with hot water so you can freshen up and a pot of tea too. You look like you could use a strong cup."

"I'd appreciate both very much."

Offering a genuine smile of gratitude, Chasity set her bonnet upon the bed. A bit of her apprehension dissolved. For all of her gruff appearance, the proprietress wasn't a curmudgeon after all.

"Well, don't you get used to it. My two maids of all work have enough to do. Water for washing and tea is kept hot in the kitchen for you to fetch yourself." With that, she marched away, her substantial girth causing her to waddle and the floor to creak.

Chasity closed the door behind her, then leaned her forehead against the wooden panel and closed her eyes.

This was real.

She'd been dismissed.

This small chamber was home for now, be it a few hours or days or weeks.

Inhaling a bracing lungful of air, she turned in a small circle, at once thankful she had a roof over her head and would have food to eat but also worried how she would find employment without a reference if she opted to stay in London.

A ragged sob forced its way past her lips, and she stuffed a fist to her mouth.

Where are you, God? Why did you let this happen to me?

It was futile. The tears Chasity had suppressed all morning surged up her throat and pooled, stinging and hot, in her eyes.

She sank onto the lumpy settee, and head in her hands, gave vent to her grief. Tears of fright and uncertainty clogged her throat and streamed from her eyes.

She cried about the injustice of her situation and the plight of women in general, which gave them so few choices in life. She wept because she was alone, and at this moment, Chasity yearned for a family she could flee to. Someone who would take her in, no questions asked, and accept and love her. She sobbed because she didn't know what to do...where to go.

And mostly, Chasity wept because the tiny, secret dream she'd harbored of a life with Aston had disintegrated to ashes.

FIFTEEN

I should've told you, Aston. I shouldn't have been a poltroon and hidden the truth from you, drowning my cowardice and guilt with spirits. Your parents didn't perish in a boating accident. Father thought that falsehood would be easier for you to bear. Scott and Elly were killed by poachers while out riding—or so my father has always maintained. There wasn't an inquiry, and I confess, I've had my doubts these many years. Scott had quarreled with the viscount and meant to take you and your mother and leave England. Father never approved of Elly, but make no mistake, he wanted you. You know, the spare heir since I refused to wed again after Margaret took her own life. I couldn't impose that misery on myself or another woman even to spare you. I regret much about my wasted life, but mostly that you were also a casualty of my father's calculations and scheming. Forgive me.

~The Honorable Conley Terramier in
a sealed letter to his nephew, Aston Terramier
Kept by his solicitor until the time of Conley's death

Upper Clapton Street
Mrs. Longsdon's Lodging House
24 August 1818 - near midnight

Barely able to keep his eyes open after a sleepless night and having spent the last several hours futilely searching for Chasity, Aston climbed the stairs to his apartments. Head hanging, Roi trailed behind him, the poor dog as exhausted as his master after the chaotic past day and a half.

Tomorrow, Aston would return to Balderbrook's Institution for Genteel Ladies and question Gibney. He'd met Bexon, sent to retrieve the magistrate, on the road, but the groom hadn't seen Chasity. He'd suggested Aston try several merchants where Gibney was to purchase the school's weekly supplies.

All of those locations had been dead ends. Where Gibney had disappeared to in London, Aston could only imagine. The man probably took the rare opportunity to dally a bit at a pub and quaff back a few ales. Mayhap even seek female company.

Aston didn't blame him for taking advantage of the occasion. Mrs. Crenshaw was a demanding employer.

Nonetheless, running into the magistrate on the road to London saved Aston a call or summons. Though it meant a slight delay in pursuing Chasity, he'd given the magistrate his statement right there. The man took copious notes and afterward said, "I shall call upon you should I need further information, Mr. Terramier."

After unlocking his door and dragging himself inside, Aston collapsed onto his bed, still fully clothed. He'd be up before dawn searching for Chasity. Werner or Grandfather could make Uncle Conley's funeral arrangements.

Tomorrow, he'd write them and tell them that very thing.

Chasity was more important than a dead man. She was

everything, and when he found her, Aston meant to tell her exactly that. His life meant nothing without her in it.

His last thought before letting slumber take him away was of her.

Is my beloved safe?

BEFORE THE KITCHEN FIRES HAD BEEN LIT, ASTON ventured below and helped himself to a piece of bread and a slice of cheese. He also grabbed two meat pies. One for himself and one for Roi. Mrs. Longsdon would box his ears if she caught him.

Though she was hard and crusty on the outside, just like a loaf of bread fresh from the oven, she was soft, sweet, and warm on the inside. This wasn't the first time he'd availed himself of food and drink in the kitchen when the lodging house was still enshrouded in slumber's mantle.

"And just what do you think you are doing?"

Blast.

Choking on a mouth full of bread, Aston whipped around and offered a lopsided smile.

Wearing a lacy, beribboned nightcap and housecoat in an alarming shade of pink, Mrs. Longsdon glared. Arms folded above her generous bosom, she tapped her slippered toe.

"Well, Aston?"

Somewhere in the eight years he'd lodged with her, she'd begun calling him Aston when they were alone. He'd never dared address her as Pearl—her given name, however.

He lifted a forefinger, silently asking for her indulgence as he gulped half a mug of warm ale to wash down the gob wedged in his throat.

Mrs. Longsdon wasn't just asking why he was sneaking about before dawn and pilfering food. She wanted to know where he'd been. Not that it was any of her business. But as she had since she'd taken him in all those years ago, she worried after him. He'd replaced the sons she'd lost in her affections.

Finally swallowing the bread, he chuckled as he set the mug on the table beside the remainder of his hasty meal. "I vow, you scared a decade off of me."

She remained mulishly silent; those terrifying eyebrows snapped together in disapproval.

Still weary after his few restless hours of sleep, he rested a hip on the kitchen table and sighed. "My uncle died two days ago. Well, actually, it was in the early morning hours yesterday."

Swiftly, he told her the basics but left out any reference to his search for Chasity.

At once, Mrs. Longsdon's stern expression softened into compassionate folds. "And I'll bet you haven't had a decent meal in all that while, have you now?"

That was her answer to everything. A hearty meal. A strong pot of steaming tea or coffee. A few biscuits, pastries, or flaky tarts. Aston had learned long ago, that was how Mrs. Longsdon showed love. By cooking and feeding those she cared for.

Tsking and tutting under her breath, she bustled around the kitchen, lighting the stove and putting coffee on.

"Sit down, Aston. I'm not letting you leave without a full belly, even if it means I have to tie you to that chair."

Aston wasn't convinced she wouldn't actually have done so.

Her critical gaze traveled to the meat pies he'd snatched for

Roi and himself. "Am I right in supposing those pies are for that hairy beast upstairs?"

Aston gave her a chagrined grin. "One is."

"Hmph." Mrs. Longsdon shook her head, and her mobcap slipped to the side a bit. "At least you take him with you, and he doesn't disturb my lodgers."

She slapped several pieces of ham onto a skillet along with a half dozen sausages. Soon, the comforting aromas of food and coffee filled the air.

"By the by," she said, setting butter and strawberry preserves on the table. "I have a new lodger."

"Oh?" Aston asked disinterestedly, his mind fixed on finding Chasity.

He'd start by visiting Balderbrook's Institution for Genteel Ladies and speaking with the other groom. Afterward, he'd call at the Trentholms' residence again. He'd gone there yesterday, but the austere butler denied Chasity had been there. Later, Aston would check the employment registries and then the hotels and other lodging houses.

Good God, there had to be hundreds in London. It would take him weeks, and he did not have weeks. It wasn't safe for Chasity to roam London unescorted. All manner of atrocious things could happen to a young woman wandering the streets.

Aston would need assistance in finding her. Before he set out today, he'd pen brief notes to his co-investors currently in town and impose upon them to use their connections to assist with the search.

Mrs. Longsdon poured him a glass of cold milk. She plunked it on the table, causing a splash of milk to trickle down the outside of the glass. Shoving the milk in front of him, she ordered in her no-nonsense tone, "Drink it. The coffee's not ready yet."

Aston knew what battles to fight, and this wasn't one of them.

"Aye, aye." Chuckling, he saluted before obediently taking a healthy swig.

Mrs. Longsdon's mouth twitched, but heaven forbid she actually permitted a full smile at his jest.

As she turned over the ham, she reflected out loud. "She's a pretty thing. Well-mannered and obviously not riff-raff. Really, she shouldn't be staying in a lodging house alone." She twirled her oversized two-pronged fork into the air as if to emphasize her words. "I wouldn't have taken her in except a friend of my son's spoke on her behalf. It never bodes well to have single young women as tenants unless they're the only boarders one takes in."

That seemed unfair to Aston, but it made sense. Young women at a boarding house could cause all manner of issues for the landlady. Other than a pair of matronly sisters and this new female, Mrs. Longsdon's other four boarders were relatively young men.

"Perhaps you should persuade her to move to a female-only establishment," Aston said offhandedly, not giving a blacksmith's curse who the lady was or if she stayed or left. "It would ensure peace and quiet around here."

"Hmm. Mayhap." Forehead puckered and mouth turned down, she gazed out the window for an extended moment. "Asking my new tenant to leave might be best. Claudia Fairburn has a nice place several blocks south. She only takes in females, though I don't know if she has any rooms available."

Mrs. Longsdon gave Aston a too innocent look. "She says they're *much* easier to manage than male tenants."

Footsteps echoed in the corridor. The maids must be up.

Aston had never given much thought to how early they were required to rise.

What time was it?

He'd left his timepiece in his room with a still snoozing Roi.

Aston glanced outside. Gloaming shadows with the merest hint of purple and pink smeared the sky.

Not quite dawn. Mayhap half past five.

"Excuse me."

Glass at his mouth, Aston froze.

He knew that voice. That incredible, precious, beloved voice.

Chasity. She was here.

He whipped around, scarcely believing his eyes. There Chasity stood in a plain gray gown, that glorious mass of hair arranged into a neat chignon, and those blue, blue eyes wide with disbelief.

"Chasity?" He extended his hands, uncaring that Mrs. Longsdon watched them with keen interest.

A joyous smile wreathing her beloved face, Chasity stumbled forward a couple of hasty steps before she seemed to realize they weren't alone and stopped.

"Aston? What are you doing here?"

SIXTEEN

I shan't marry him. I shan't, and Mama and Papa cannot make me. Werner Terramier is a rake and a libertine. He's a horrid, smelly man with a fondness for strumpets and drink. I'm no fool. I know full well that Grandmama established a clause in my trust that I am permitted to choose my own husband. And I assuredly do not select that pasty-faced, vile, stinking drunkard. In two months, I will be five-and-twenty, and the trust reverts to me. That is why they are in such a hurry to wed me to that beastly man. I haven't avoided marriage this long to be forced into wedding a sodding bounder. I overheard my parents speaking with his grandfather. Mama and Papa want a portion of the forty thousand pounds Grandmama left me. I just need a place to stay—oh, very well, to hide— until 23 October, and then I shall petition the courts to release my trust fund. Lord Woolbury and my parents think because I'm on the shelf and not a beauty that I'd be grateful to marry for a title. How little they know me. I'd much rather remain a spinster and control my own destiny

than marry that disgusting reprobate. I mean to secret away on the mail coach tomorrow.

~ Lady Agatha Dahlzey in a secret note
to her cousin and best friend,
Ruth Glaser-Corrigan.

Mrs. Longsdon's Lodging House
Guest parlor
Fifteen minutes later

Aston was here. Right here, lounging across from Chasity in a pecan brown brocade armchair, and his was quite the most welcome, precious face she'd ever seen. Stubble covered his jaw, and weariness crinkled the corners of his eyes. Regardless, his exhaustion didn't detract in the least from his striking good looks.

She longed to run her hand through his hair and soothe the fatigue from his features.

Allowing herself the luxury of examining him as she went about preparing to pour their coffee, she smiled inwardly. It was so very good to see him. She'd been afraid she'd never set eyes upon him again, and the blood in her veins fairly sang for joy.

Her heart had plunked to her toes and then spiraled to her throat with the force of a tornado upon spying him in the kitchen. She'd come to ask for a piece of bread and cheese and perhaps an apple to take with her while she searched for a position today.

After hours of crying, she'd concluded she couldn't risk spending all of her savings on coach fare to start over somewhere. And as no magistrate had pounded upon the door during the night, intent on arresting her, Chasity prayed none would. That might make her imprudent, but perhaps Gibney hadn't been interrogated, or mayhap he'd fibbed.

Or possibly, the magistrate had been summoned for a different reason. She supposed it was too much to hope it was to arrest Mrs. Crenshaw.

Never had she imagined she'd find her heart's desire resting his slender hips against a kitchen table and chatting with their landlady.

This morning, no fire lit the salon, but the curtains had been drawn wide and the early morning sun filtered through the gleaming windows. Cozy with a homey, inviting atmosphere, the room had been decorated simply.

Several chairs in earthen shades were situated strategically around the parlor. A lush fern sat upon a table near the windows, a potted Ficus nearly six feet tall stood between two other windows, and one wall contained a shelf with an assortment of books, a chess set, and decks of cards.

The cat she'd seen yesterday on the stoop, along with a large, fluffy orange cat, lay sleeping contentedly on one of the chairs. A ray of sunshine bathed their intertwined bodies.

The salon was the perfect backdrop for the relaxed, refined man across from Chasity. His eyes, dark as the coffee she was about to pour, held the promise of something tantalizing and sent tingles up and down her spine each time she met his penetrating gaze.

Jacketless, Aston wore a jade green waistcoat, and the fabric of his fine lawn shirt pulled taut across his broad shoulders. He'd rolled his shirtsleeves to his elbows, revealing the crisp, dark brown hair covering his sculpted forearms. Never in Chasity's life would she have suspected a man's shoulders and arms could be so...*so*...appealing.

Of course, he might've just come from months of deprivation and imprisonment in Newgate's deepest bowels, and

Chasity would still think him the most handsome man she knew.

Love did that. Made everyone incomparable to the one who held your heart.

The sky seemed a more vivid shade of blue. Flowers smelled more fragrant. The sun shone brighter, and everywhere one looked, there was something to be grateful for or to enjoy.

Surely the Good Lord had His hand in this incredible coincidence. That out of all of the boarding houses Chasity might've chosen to stay at, she picked the same one where Aston rented rooms.

Or had Gibney had something to do with that? Had the groom known?

"You are well?" Aston asked solicitously as Chasity poured him a cup of coffee.

"Quite well, thank you." She hated this polite, stilted small talk when they'd spoken so easily together before.

She paused, a hand hovering over the sugar bowl.

How did Aston like his coffee?

She smiled self-consciously. "I regret don't know how you take your coffee, Aston."

How could she love this man beyond all else and not know something so trivial? She didn't know his favorite color, favorite food, if he had any siblings, what he enjoyed reading, if he had any hobbies...

The truth of it was that she knew very little about Aston Terramier other than that he danced divinely, and she'd fallen hopelessly, madly, and irrevocably in love with him. Her heart had been his since that day he'd taken her in his arms and whisked her around the ballroom floor.

"Two lumps. No milk," Aston responded with a lazy, sideways smile. "And you?"

"Me?" Chasity gave him a startled glance.

"How do you take your coffee?" He slung an ankle over his knee and idly tapped his fingers on a muscular thigh. Not that Chasity made a habit of noticing men's sinewy thighs. But the buff-colored pantaloons left little to the imagination.

Aston had very nice thighs indeed.

"I don't drink coffee. That is, I've never had the opportunity. I believe the first coffee in England came from Turkey, did it not?"

He lifted his cup to his molded lips and blew softly. "Yes, a fellow named Daniel Edwards was a trader in Turkish goods. Supposedly, with the assistance of a servant, he established the first coffee house in England. Now coffee is produced in several countries other than Turkey."

Raising the teacup to her nose, Chasity inhaled deeply. "It does possess the most delicious aroma."

"Some varieties are quite bitter until you become accustomed to the strong taste." Aston waved those long fingers toward the coffee pot. "I'd suggest you prepare yours the same way you would your tea."

"A healthy portion of milk and two lumps of sugar it is then." She plunked the lumps into his cup and hers as well. Grinning, she lifted the small milk pitcher. "I actually prefer cream in my tea like the Americans, but it's not *de rigueur* in English Society."

Stirring her coffee, Chasity slid her glance toward the three-inch opening between the door and door jamb. She could hear the maids moving in and out of the dining room down the hall if she concentrated. They spoke in subdued tones, laughing every now and again.

"Good morning, Miss Hilda. Miss Joan," one of the maids greeted. "The stewed prunes will be out in a moment."

"Bring plenty, girl," bellowed one of the older women,

obviously hard of hearing. "Neither my sister nor I have had a movement in two days."

Chasity's gaze careened to Aston.

Jollity danced in his eyes, and his lips twitched.

"Well, living with several other people can be most entertaining." Chasity knew that to be the truth from having been raised in a foundling home and working in a girls' seminary for several years.

She took a sip of her coffee. True, the taste was strong, but the sugar and milk made it quite palatable. It was actually rather good and somewhat soothing. She took another swallow as she considered what she'd overheard as she came down the corridor to the kitchen earlier.

Perhaps you should persuade her to move to a female-only establishment. It would ensure peace and quiet around here.

She hadn't realized the muffled male voice was Aston's.

Asking my new tenant to leave might be best.

Was Mrs. Longsdon going to evict Chasity already?

Simply because she was female? Or because she was unmarried?

But she'd clearly heard the maid address two female boarders as *Miss* but moments before. Well, there was nothing to be done about that at this moment.

Upon learning Chasity and Aston knew each other and that he'd been searching for her since her abrupt departure from Balderbrook's Institution for Genteel Ladies yesterday, Mrs. Longsdon had insisted they eat breakfast in the privacy of the salon rather than the dining room. With the door cracked for propriety, naturally.

Wise woman, Mrs. Longsdon had swiftly deduced they had much to discuss, and such a conversation was better held in privacy, despite her strict rules about eating in the dining room. That she doted on Aston was apparent from the affectionate glances she sent his way, and he returned her regard.

"I've lived here eight years," he remarked. "You won't find a better cook than Mrs. Longsdon in all of London, I vow."

"The food smells divine."

Chasity's stomach rumbled loudly. She hadn't eaten since yesterday morning. She'd fallen asleep after her cry, and if the promised tea tray and hot water had been sent up, Chasity hadn't been aware.

Offering Aston an apologetic smile, she picked up a piece of toast. She took a bite and nearly sighed in delight.

Had anything ever tasted so delicious?

She finished the toast in four large, unladylike bites, and without a jot of remorse, helped herself to another thick slice. Smeared in strawberry preserves, the toast was heavenly.

Aston rose and, in a few long strides, reached the door and closed it.

Intent on filling her hollow stomach, Chasity eyed him but continued to eat.

He returned, but instead of taking the seat he'd just vacated, he sat down beside her on the settee.

Chasity's heart fluttered like a caged sparrow's wings when he took her hand. She stared at their hands, his dark and lightly sprinkled with hair, and hers so much fairer and smaller.

"Chasity, please forgive me for not being there as I had promised you yesterday morning. I regret you had to endure that awful inquisition without me by your side."

She shook her head. "But—"

"Please, darling. Let me finish." Aston ran his thumb over her knuckles and gave her one of his devastating smiles.

Her hunger for food vanished, and another kind of hunger, foreign and giddy, ignited in her middle.

"My uncle died. That's what the note was about that I received at the Trentholms'."

He pressed two fingers to the bridge of his nose and closed his eyes for a heartbeat. Chasity had never known anyone who had died, but she could imagine the anguish.

"He passed in the early morning, and I had to scour London for hours to find my cousin."

Aston had been with his uncle when he passed, but the man's own son had not?

"How awful for you. I'm sorry." She laid her hand on Aston's firm knee. At her touch, the hard flesh rippled beneath her palm. "Were you close to your uncle?"

"At one time. My uncle was a good man but, unfortunately, a weak one. My grandfather ran roughshod over him, and my uncle coped with his misery by tipping the bottle." Aston lifted a shoulder and pulled a rueful face. "Sadly, Conley's fondness for drink sent him to an early grave. He'd just passed his fifty-second year."

"Your grandfather has lost two sons. That's tragic by any measure." An awful circumstance for any parent to endure. "Has he any other children?"

"No. There's just my cousin Werner and me now. He's two years my senior, and unfortunately, has had as great an affection for the bottle as his father had."

Realizing her hand still rested upon Aston's marble-like thigh, Chasity moved it to her lap. Aston still cradled her other hand in his, and she felt absolutely no compulsion to withdraw that hand as well.

A comfortable stillness settled around them, punctuated by the rhythmic *tick-tock* of the clock and impressive feline purring. Chasity and Aston sat in companionable silence for a few moments.

A carriage rumbled past outside, and Aston stirred.

Not only had breakfast grown cold, Mrs. Longsdon didn't seem the sort to condone perfectly good food going to waste.

"After you left Mrs. Crenshaw's office yesterday, several matters were set straight," Aston said.

Chasity brought her attention back to him. She'd prefer not to discuss yesterday's ugliness, but there was no help for it. "Such as?"

"Mrs. Crenshaw forged my resignation letter and replaced my employment contract with another counterfeit." Shaking his head, Aston scratched his unshaven jaw. "She wasn't even clever in her machinations. I don't know how she thought she could possibly succeed with her scheme."

"I suspect she became quite desperate and stopped thinking clearly." Though Chasity couldn't summon sympathy for the woman, neither could she rejoice in her downfall. She hadn't been raised to gloat over other's misfortunes, even if they brought the calamity on themselves.

"I've already spoken to the magistrate, Chasity, and I expect you shall be fully acquitted of the false charges."

She loved hearing her name on Aston's lips.

Such a small thing, a silly thing, but it warmed her very soul.

"Thank you, Aston."

Did that mean she would soon be reinstated as assistant headmistress?

She should have been overjoyed, but instead, Chasity felt rather lost and adrift. The things that had mattered most to her were no longer a priority. She wasn't sure she wanted to return to Balderbrook's Institution for Genteel Ladies and take up her former life. Granted, it had been less than a full day since she'd left, but that life, that of a spinster teacher secure in her drab role, wasn't what Chasity wanted any longer.

The man sitting beside her, holding her hand, was what she longed for. To have a future with him.

Aston gave her fingers a soft squeeze. "When you left yesterday, and I couldn't find you, I determined something."

Canting her head, Chasity searched his dear face. "And what was that?"

"That if I found you, I'd never let you go again."

It sounded like... Did he mean?

Was it possible?

Dare she hope?

What about Italy?

Chasity bit her lower lip to keep the questions pelting the back of her teeth from spewing forth. Excitement, anticipation, exhilaration, and longing cavorted in her mind and heart, creating an impossible tangle of emotions.

She tamped down the eagerness swirling through her. *Don't jump to conclusions*, she admonished inwardly in her sternest schoolmistress tone. After all, just a few minutes ago, she'd heard Aston telling Mrs. Longsdon that it might very well be a good idea to have her move to a different boarding house.

"Do you understand what I am saying, Chasity?"

"Didn't you just tell Mrs. Longsdon it would be a good idea for me to find a different place to lodge?"

Aston's brow crinkled in befuddlement before comprehension dawned. He grinned. "I didn't know she was talking about you, else I never would have made such a preposterous suggestion."

"But I thought you were going to Italy." Chasity couldn't let herself trust in her heart of hearts what she desperately wanted to believe Aston was saying.

That he wanted to be with her. That he wanted to marry her.

Aston's smoldering gaze caught hers and held it captive. Slowly, he raised her hand to his mouth and placed a kiss on the back of it. Then he pressed his mouth to her palm and finally brushed his lips across the inside of her wrist.

"Only if you go with me," he said before his mouth enveloped hers.

SEVENTEEN

Miss Noble, I fear we have done you a grave disservice, and I must apologize. Once the magistrate arrived and explained that Mrs. Crenshaw could expect a more lenient sentence if she cooperated, she confessed all. I speak on behalf of the other benefactors and the board when I say we welcome you back to Balderbrook's Institution for Genteel Ladies. We would be honored to have someone with your integrity and loyalty as the new headmistress.

~ Lady Jane Balderbrook in a letter
to Miss Chasity Noble
Entrusted to the care of
Aston Terramier for delivery

Still in Mrs. Longsdon's guest salon
Several delicious minutes later

Aston nibbled Chasity's earlobe, delighting in the way she sighed and arched her neck to give him greater access to the delicate ivory flesh. As always, she smelled of lemons and flowers. Perhaps peonies or jasmine. No connoisseur of women's scents, he couldn't identify the specific blossoms. Nonetheless, the combination was wholly intoxicating.

Kissing her, even with the door closed wasn't wise. Mrs. Longsdon or one of the boarders could intrude at any moment. Though Aston intended to make Chasity his wife, if she would have him, he wouldn't have her reputation sullied.

With a regretful half growl, half sigh, he angled away from her.

"Minx. I cannot resist you."

Her lashes half-moons upon her gentle sloping cheekbones, and her lips red from his kisses, she was a temptress. *His* temptress. Or so he prayed.

Aston ran his knuckle down Chasity's smooth cheek. "As much as I'd like to continue kissing you, sweetheart, we risk interruption."

Her eyelashes slowly fluttered open, and her mouth swept upward into a radiant smile that lit the entire room. Such adoration shone in her eyes that it humbled Aston. Made him want to take her in his arms and swing her around and around while shouting to the world that he loved her.

"And our breakfast has grown cold," she said impishly, pointing her gaze to the two plates of barely touched food.

Affecting affront, he pressed an arm across his chest. "Do my kisses mean so little that the promise of food erases them from my darling's memory?"

"Of course not, you simpleton." Giggling, Chasity shook her head. "But a lady hardly discusses such matters."

Aston swooped in for one last lingering kiss, then moved to the armchair once more. Best to remove himself from such a temptation.

Sprout, the calico, raised her head and gave him a sleepy stare before snuggling with her brother and falling back to sleep. When was the last time either of those lazy cats had caught anything other than a tasty morsel deliberately dropped beneath the table by one of the Smithersfort sisters?

"We'd best remedy that, or we'll be in the suds with our landlady," he said, popping a bite of sausage into his mouth. "And tomorrow is cinnamon bun day. I'd hate to be in her bad graces and be denied several of the scrumptious rolls."

With a happy nod and a grin, Chasity took up her plate.

Rather than follow suit, Aston leaned forward and rested his elbows on his knees while cupping his chin with is hands. He could watch this remarkable woman all day and never grow bored.

He wanted to marry her, but there were a few details he needed to sort out before he formally proposed. For instance, informing his meddlesome grandfather that there would be no match between Aston and Saphira Finch-Hatten.

God only knew how far that rumor had spread already. He wouldn't put it past the viscount to post the betrothal in the news sheets without consulting Aston. Though he supposed Werner's upcoming nuptials were sufficient to temporarily placate Grandfather's ambitions for an heir.

"I shall be away for most of the day, Chasity. I have a few urgent errands to run, and I must also help with my uncle's funeral arrangements." Now that he'd found Chasity, he could honor his uncle's request. "I can look in at Balderbrook's Institution for you if you wish."

A forkful of ham raised halfway to her mouth, she paused. "Yes, please. I left so abruptly. I would appreciate it if you would give them my forwarding address."

"I would be happy to."

Frowning, she shook her head. "The students and staff must be in quite a dither. Losing their headmistress and assistant headmistress within mere hours."

"Lady Balderbrook has appointed Mrs. Ramsbottom as the interim headmistress." Chasity needed to know about the arrangement, but would it wound her further?

Placing her still full fork on her plate, she nodded and glanced out the window. "Stella will do well. She's always aspired to a higher position. I am glad she has the opportunity to demonstrate her competence."

"I'm positive once the inquiry is completed, you will be offered your position once more. Perhaps even that of the headmistress."

Is that still what she wanted?

Or could Aston persuade her to take a different course with her life? He wasn't titled, but he made a respectable living. And though they mightn't live a luxurious lifestyle, they would be comfortable. He could envision them in a cozy house, several children running about, and every night, the last thing he would do before wrapping her in his arms and falling asleep would be to tell her how much he loved her.

After giving his lady a few lessons in love, that was.

Based on the enticing kisses they'd shared and the joy shining in Chasity's eyes, he was willing to wager everything that mattered to him that she was ready to become Mrs. Aston Terramier.

"I have another position I'd have you fill, however, Chasity."

Chasity's gaze flew to meet his. "And would that position have something to do with your trip to Italy?"

"It could." Aston raised his eyebrows and grinned.

"I speak and read Italian fluently," she said, a flirtatious twinkle in her eyes.

"I do not, which is all the more reason you must accompany me." He leaned forward and flicked a silky curl. "Have supper with me tonight? I know of a charming little eatery."

He added buying an engagement ring to his list of things to do today. And by George, he would not wait until he was out of mourning for Uncle Conley to marry this incomparable woman.

"Of course, though what I'll do with myself all day, I cannot imagine." She caught sight of a desk nestled in the corner. "I suppose I could catch up on my correspondence." Chasity angled that cloud of flaxen hair toward the desk. "Are there writing supplies? I haven't any with me."

"I have everything you need," Aston offered. "I'll make sure what you require is sent to your room."

He'd been on the verge of offering to let her use his chamber, but Mrs. Longsdon would disapprove. "Perhaps you could walk Roi for me later? I cannot take him with me today."

"I'd love to. A bit of exercise would do me good too."

Aston rose then. He'd best be about his business if he wanted to return in time to dine with Chasity. Drawing her to her feet, he pulled her near until their thighs brushed, and he could see the flecks in her eyes.

"I love you, Chasity. I didn't mean to, but you've become the dearest, most precious thing in the world to me."

Again, that blinding smile wreathed her face, and her eyes went soft with emotion.

"I love you too, Aston. Impossibly so."

She didn't blush or cast her gaze downward in timidity. She spoke the words with confidence and strength.

He kissed her forehead. "Until tonight then, my love."

With a final glance behind him, treasuring the sight of

Chasity standing there gazing after him with love shining in her eyes, Aston quit the salon.

He needed to pen a note to his grandfather and arrange for a meeting this afternoon. It was far past time he put his grandfather in his place once and for all.

EIGHTEEN

I shall call promptly at four o'clock this afternoon. We can discuss Uncle Conley's final arrangements then. There are other serious matters that I wish to speak to you about as well. Assure that Werner is present too.

~ Aston Terramier in a cryptic note
to Viscount Woolbury

London
Berkeley Square
Sutton House
25 August 1818 - half past four in the afternoon

With a frustrated glance toward the mahogany bracket clock, Aston paced his grandfather's study. Almost forty minutes since Lowell had shown him to the office, and the viscount had yet to put in an appearance.

Leave it to the old man to refuse to cooperate. He always had to be in control, to have the last word. Always. Well, not today. Not anymore, if Aston accomplished what he set out to do. And by God, he would succeed.

His attention shifted to his cousin, looking far worse for wear.

Unshaven, his neckcloth stained and partially untied, Werner slouched in an armchair. He wore the same clothes Aston had found him in the night Uncle Conley had died. From his rumpled, unkempt appearance, he'd been pished nonstop for days. A glass of brandy dangled from his left hand —his second since tottering in half an hour ago.

"For God's sake, sit down, Aston." Werner took a noisy slurp. "I'm bloody exhausted just watching you pace back and forth."

As impossible as it seemed, Werner looked even unhealthier than he had mere days ago.

"Werner, did you see another physician? I don't mean to press the issue, but you don't look well." Mayhap the Earl of Clarendon or one of the other co-investors could recommend a physician. One who did more than bleed their patients.

"So nice of you to be concerned, Cuz." Werner belched and then chuckled. After draining his glass, he glanced around dazedly. He skewered the empty brandy decanter with a nasty glare. "He's hidden the good stuff from me."

"You've had enough. Far too much, in truth." Aston plucked the glass from his cousin's limp fingers. "And you didn't answer my question. Have you seen another physician?"

Werner kicked his legs out before him and, with a hearty sigh, laced his fingers together atop his belly and closed his eyes.

"I did indeed," he grunted. "More than one, truth be told."

"And?"

The study door flew open, sparing Werner from answering.

Grandfather stomped across the room, the Corinthian blue and beige Aubusson carpeting muffling his heavy, uneven tread. He leveled Aston and Werner thunderous scowls in turn. Cursing foully beneath his breath, Grandfather tossed the paper he held onto his desk.

Even in his youth, Milton Terramier, Viscount Woolbury, hadn't been an attractive man. Bowlegged and practically chinless, he rather resembled an oversized bird or mayhap a tortoise. At six-and-seventy, bald, with bad teeth, and gone to fat, he was even less so.

"Your horse-faced betrothed has run away, Werner," he snapped as if it were Werner's fault. Which, if his affianced had ever met Werner, it likely was. "Ungrateful, homely chit. At her age and with an arse as wide as a barn door, you'd think she'd be grateful to become a future viscountess."

Prying an eyelid open, Werner smirked. "S'pose that means the weddings off then."

"Until I can find another bride with a heavy dowry, it is." Grandfather practically gnashed what remained of his yellowed teeth.

Werner lifted a fist. "Huzzah. One prayer answered."

"Bah. You always were an ungrateful wretch." Woolbury cut the air with a sharp gesture as he wedged himself into the leather chair behind his monstrous desk. "There's no shortage of gels eager to marry themselves a title. The older and uglier, the more desperate they are. That's how I found your grandmother. Two-and thirty, a lazy eye, and a face her mother couldn't even profess to love."

Unconscionable cad.

Aston literally bit his tongue to keep from telling his grandfather what a revolting piece of excrement he was. No woman should be spoken of so disparagingly. Losing his temper before he'd had his say wasn't the way he intended this meeting to go. Nevertheless, that didn't stop him from sending his grandfather a murderous scowl and wishing him to hell's deepest level.

Seemingly oblivious to Aston's glower, the viscount steepled his hands, then tapped his fingertips together. "Truth be told, the wench hightailing to kingdom come might work to our benefit. Some of the *ton* believes it was crass to continue with the wedding when your father had just died."

"It was rather," Aston put in. "Crass, that is. Uncle Conley deserves a modicum of respect after the unhappy life he lived."

Other than narrowing his eyes, Grandfather didn't respond.

Hmm, he was behaving exceptionally genial today. Notably, after he'd just received upsetting news. Which meant he was scheming something devious.

Grandfather screwed his face into a calculating expression. "Yes, yes, indeed. A few weeks, a couple of months perchance might play in our favor."

He rubbed his hands together, much like a villain celebrating his crime.

With a disinterested sniff, Werner closed his eyes once more, effectively dismissing his grandfather. That was a first. Usually, he groveled like a sycophant toady to please the domineering old sot.

"Except," Werner drawled. "It won't make any difference when I wed."

He laughed, a half-demented, half-derisive chortle that raised Aston's nape hairs.

"What's that?" He had their grandfather's attention and Aston's too. "What twaddle are you blathering now, Werner?"

"It seems, dearest Grandpapa, I have the creeping paralysis and am as sterile as the gelding I ride. Caught the French pox years ago from some faceless whore I cannot remember."

Sweet Jesus on Sunday.

He released a humorless laugh. "Didn't even know I was infected. The physician says that's the case sometimes. I've waited too long for treatment." He flicked his fingers near his groin. "These loins won't be producing any future viscounts."

Though he'd brought the calamity on himself, Aston's heart wrenched for his cousin.

Werner covered his eyes with a bent elbow.

To hide his shame? Tears? Remorse?

An oppressive, pregnant silence descended, cocooning the study in despondency.

His mind balking at what Werner's confession meant, Aston clasped his hands behind his back, the nails cutting half-moons into his palms.

Bollocks. Bollocks. Bollocks!

He couldn't even permit his mind to formulate the truth.

The godawful, horrendous truth.

"I don't believe you," Grandfather blustered. "You are bluffing. You're fabricating poppycock, Werner, so that you don't have to wed." He pounded the desk with his fist, rattling the inkwell. "I shan't have it. I'll have you examined by my physician."

"I already did," came Werner's muffled response due to his arm partially covering his face. "This is one time, old man, that you cannot bend me to your will."

"How dare you?" the viscount seethed, yet something near panic flashed in his watery eyes.

Werner lowered his arm and leveled their grandfather an acrid stare. "My days are literally numbered, and I am not doing your bidding any longer. I intend to live the remaining scant days of my life in peace."

Good for you, cousin.

He pushed to his feet, moving like a ninety-year-old arthritic decrepit instead of a man just past his thirtieth year. Eyes red-rimmed and cheeks hollow, he faced Aston and fashioned a wan smile.

Aston's gut clenched in sorrow and pity.

"I have always admired you for standing up to him." He jerked his head toward their thunderstruck—no, fuming— grandfather. "Don't ever stop, Aston. Don't ever become a malleable, spineless sot like me. He'll destroy you like he did your parents, my parents, and me."

With that, he left the room on unsteady legs, leaving the door gaping open behind him.

The clock *tick-tocked* three times before the viscount cleared his throat, then cleared it heartily again.

Werner had put the old goat off his stride. Bless him for having more courage than he gave himself credit for.

"Well then, Aston, my boy, it's up to you to ensure the title doesn't die out." Grandfather's countenance transformed into beguiling solicitousness. "I have just the bride for you. I've spoken to her parents, and they are most eager for the match. She's—"

"No."

"No? *No?*" His voice rising in pitch on the last word, Grandfather spluttered and turned crimson. "What do you mean no? It's already been arranged. I cannot go back on my word."

"No. I will not marry Saphira Finch-Hatten." A satisfied grin pulling his mouth upward, Aston crossed his arms, thoroughly enjoying having flummoxed his grandfather.

That took the wind out of the viscount's sails. His grizzled eyebrows slashed together, and irritation flattened his lips. "I suppose Werner told you of my plans."

"He did. I shall choose my own bride. In fact, I already have."

Grandfather's keen raptor's gaze fixed on Aston. "Who?"

"No one you know, thank God. If what Werner says about his health is true, Grandfather, then I shall eventually become your heir. I've never wanted the title, and I still don't."

Aston perched on the arm of a chair and folded his arms again.

"Regardless," he said, "we don't always get what we want in life, do we? Some people manipulate and scheme and blackmail and bribe and coerce and bully, and even commit murder, to get what *they* desire."

Grandfather went perfectly still, the way an animal does when cornered by prey and aware they face death. He swallowed reflexively, his gaze darting back and forth.

Well, Aston had his answer as surely as if the viscount had confessed.

He hadn't wanted to believe what he'd read in the short note delivered by Uncle Conley's solicitor's clerk while he'd been out yesterday. He'd found the sealed letter on his table upon awakening this morning. Uncle Conley had suspected his father had killed his brother and sister-in-law to ensure they didn't take Aston away.

Aston rose and, taking measured steps, crossed the room until he was directly before his grandfather's desk. How many times had he faced the viscount across the vast expanse of the piece of furniture, as a small, terrified lad and dozens of times since? Always with the older man confident of his power and authority.

Not anymore.

The title mattered so little to him; Aston would gladly

leave this house and never give the viscountcy another thought.

His grandfather eyed him warily. A first for the curmudgeon.

"I don't know what nonsensical drivel you are talking about, Aston," he blustered.

Aston removed Uncle Conley's letter and dropped it, still folded, in front of his grandfather. "Did you have my parents killed to keep me in England?"

Every ounce of color drained from the viscount's face as perspiration simultaneously beaded his upper lip and forehead. He groped in his pocket for his handkerchief. As he mopped his face, he fearfully eyed the folded rectangle like one would a cobra about to strike.

"I'd bet my inheritance that you did." Palms flat on the desk, Aston leaned forward. "I'd also bet there's someone who knows exactly what you did. Someone you paid to do your dirty work."

Grandfather's gaze shifted to the left. More confirmation, the bloody sod.

Was the murderer still alive?

Likely, given the viscount's anxious reaction.

Aston straightened. "Have I mentioned that three of my co-investors in the Italian marble quarry, Viscounts Sethwick and Warrick, and the Earl of Ramsbury once worked for the Home Office? They have the most extraordinary way of turning up information. Information that people would prefer to remain...*private*."

Sagging into his chair, Grandfather deflated like a broken balloon. He appeared old, and broken, and surprisingly fragile.

Regardless, Aston felt not a jot of pity or compassion.

"What do you want, Aston?"

A considerable concession that. The old buzzard hadn't

outright admitted his guilt, but Grandfather might as well have done.

"I want you to take yourself off to that remote hunting lodge you never use in the Borderlands and stay there the rest of your miserable days. I want you to leave Werner and me alone and never interfere in our lives again. Or so help me God, I will have the matter of my parents' deaths investigated."

The viscount gave a weak nod. "I'll go. By the end of the week."

"No. You'll leave immediately after Uncle Conley's funeral, which is tomorrow afternoon at four. I've made the arrangements. I suggest you have your valet begin packing at once."

Aston pointed to the inkwell and quill. "Write a letter to your solicitor granting me full proxy to act on your behalf. Werner will need medical care, and I don't want you to have any excuse for showing your face in London again."

Oddly, the rage that Aston had thought he'd feel didn't rise up. Yes, there was disgust, and a righteous sense of anger encompassed him. But this pathetic excuse for a human being wasn't worth his hatred.

Shortly, Aston tucked the newly-penned authorization into his pocket. "A man with your power and wealth could've made a difference in this world, Grandfather. Instead, you've wasted your life manipulating and scheming."

The old man didn't answer, but curled his mouth into a belligerent snarl. No remorse or regret shone in his eyes either.

"If I inherit, and I pray I do not, but if I do, I intend to use the title to benefit others in any way I can." Aston pulled his cuffs down and marched to the door. "Now, I'm going to ask the most remarkable, intelligent, kind woman I know to be my wife."

NINETEEN

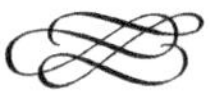

I am to accompany Lord and Lady Ceddes and their children to a country house party. Always before, they've left their offspring in my care as they gallivant about. I can only think this is their last hurrah before sending the children away to school next month. They haven't even done me the courtesy of providing me notice of my employment termination or mentioned writing me a recommendation. I intend to promptly rectify those oversights. Perhaps at the house party when they are in a reasonable frame of mind. I have no notion what goes on at these types of gatherings, but as I'll be supervising my charges, I needn't worry overly much. I shall miss Pomeroy, Merrilee, and Amaris. These past eight years have been a challenge, to be sure, but I love the children. Change is never easy, but I look forward to my next position, wherever that may be. Perhaps I shall apply to Balderbrook's Institution for Genteel Ladies after all.

~ Miss Purity Mayfield in a hasty letter
to Miss Chasity Noble.

Mrs. Longsdon's Lodging House
25 August 1818 - early evening

For the umpteenth time, Chasity glanced out the window. The day had dragged by with interminable slowness. Even walking Roi twice and writing several letters hadn't made the time pass more swiftly.

She'd eaten a tasty luncheon of shepherd's pie in the dining room. Only Mrs. Longsdon, spinster sisters Hilda and Joan Smithersfort, and a retired and widowed cleric, Wallace Appleyard, had also been present.

Chasity had endured a polite interrogation by the other three lodgers. She'd kept her answers brief and vague. She'd been raised in a foundling home. She was a teacher between positions at present. She was grateful to have found such pleasant lodgings.

When it became apparent she wasn't divulging any deep secrets or sharing gossip, they left her to herself. Except for Mrs. Longsdon's penetrating looks, that was. That woman was too astute by far.

Wandering to the salon's window again, Chasity gazed past the heavy draperies. Still no Aston. He wasn't precisely tardy. After all, he hadn't explicitly said when he'd return.

Across the room, the Smithersfort sisters dozed in adjacent armchairs, each with a cat asleep on her lap. Their sonorous snores competing for dominance made it impossible to read anyway.

The elderly ladies had lived at the lodging house since being put out of their home by their nephew five years ago. Despite his aged aunts having lived there for three decades, after inheriting the house from his father, he'd decided to sell the place.

The world was full of evil and selfish people.

True, but there were also decent, honest, and kind people. People like Aston, Mrs. Shepherd, and Mrs. Longsdon. Aston had told Chasity how the landlady had taken him when he'd had no means to pay her.

Chasity had taken extra care with her appearance. She'd changed into her forest green gown and styled her hair in a new fashion, leaving a few curls to frame her face. She even wore the silver cross Mrs. Shepherd had given her.

The book of poetry she'd been trying to read lay face down on the settee where Aston had so thoroughly kissed her this morning.

She touched her fingertips to her mouth.

Had it really only been this morning?

He hadn't exactly asked her to marry him, but surely he'd alluded to it.

A trip to Italy.

He had a position to offer her.

He loved her.

A horrific thought speared Chasity, and she clenched the curtain fabric. Her breath stalled as her palms turned clammy. Surely, he didn't mean to ask her to be his mistress.

No. She shook her head. Absolutely not. A man of Aston's character would not insult her so. She dismissed the idea as quickly as the nasty thing had intruded.

A moment later, Mrs. Longsdon bustled into the salon. "Dinner will be served soon."

Was it nearly seven already?

The Smithersfort sisters bolted upright upon hearing that. Both cats awoke with a perturbed yowl. With the stiff, labored movements of the elderly, they put the cats down and rose.

"I'm famished," Miss Hilda declared. She pointed her nose into the air and sniffed. "Is that pot roast I smell?"

Hands clasped atop her belly, Mrs. Longsdon beamed. "It is indeed."

Miss Joan slipped her knobby fingers into the crook of her sister's elbow. "No one makes a pot roast better than Mrs. Longsdon, my dear. Are you sure you won't have a plate?"

Chasity smiled but shook her head. "No. I shall wait for Mr. Terramier."

The sisters shuffled from the room, chatting excitedly about supper.

Mrs. Longsdon straightened the pillows on the chairs, then clasped her hands in front of her. "I'll put a plate aside for you and Mr. Terramier just in case he's delayed."

Before Chasity could remark on the woman's kindness, Aston strode into the parlor carrying a huge bouquet of flowers.

As always, her heart gave a gleeful skip. Aston had shaved and changed his clothes since this morning. Though his attire was unadorned, there was no mistaking the quality of the garments or the man wearing them. Aston might be a dance master and music teacher, but he bore himself like an aristocrat.

Mrs. Longsdon raised an imperious brow.

"Well, it seems I shan't have to prepare a plate after all." She eyed the flowers. "I'll just get you a vase for your bouquet, Miss Noble."

"Ah, but they're not for her. They are for you, Pearl." Aston held them toward the flabbergasted woman.

She put a hand to her ample chest. "Me?" Tears clouded her eyes. "But whatever for?"

Aston leaned down and kissed her cheek. "Because you deserve them. I don't tell you often enough how much I appreciate you and all you have done for me." He gave her a cheeky wink. "And I know how to keep the best cook in London happy."

If Chasity hadn't already been hopelessly in love with him, her heart would've become his at that moment.

"Oh, posh. Enough of your flattery." Mrs. Longsdon accepted the flowers with the reverence one might hold a priceless tiara. A smile wreathing her flushed face, she gave Chasity a knowing look. "Aston's a fine catch, he is."

Chasity wasn't sure how to respond. After all, they weren't formally betrothed. "He is the finest of gentlemen, to be sure."

Aston grasped Mrs. Longsdon's shoulders and aimed her toward the door. "I require a few moments of privacy with Miss Noble."

"I'll just put these in water and call the others to dinner." Before she closed the door, she said, "Take your time. I'll ensure you're not interrupted."

Was this the same woman who had warned Chasity just yesterday that she wasn't to have any gentleman callers?

As soon as the door clicked shut, Aston drew her into his arms. Several minutes passed as they explored one another's mouths. Winding her arms about his neck, Chasity gave herself over to her love and desire for him.

At last, he drew back, his breathing ragged. "Forgive me for returning so late. My errands took longer than I anticipated."

"It's of no matter," she replied rather breathlessly, still trying to recover from the sizzling kisses they'd just shared.

"I have two letters for you." He passed them to her, and while she cracked the first seal, he moved about the salon, lighting the lamps. A soft glow filled the room, and she realized he'd lit the lamps many times before. This had been his home for years.

Chasity scanned the letter from Lady Balderbrook and glanced up as Aston returned to her. "I've been offered the position of headmistress at Balderbrook's Institution for Genteel Ladies. I must say, that was rather swifter than I'd anticipated."

Grinning, he plucked the letter from her fingers and tossed it onto a nearby table. "Regretfully, you shall have to decline."

"Perhaps." Quirking a brow, she eyed him. "Perhaps not."

"Perhaps *not*?" With a playful growl, Aston caught her to him and nuzzled her neck.

Chasity giggled. "Yes. I haven't quite decided yet. At present, I don't have a better offer."

"I fear my wife will be far too busy adjusting to married life to be a headmistress."

She froze, her breath suspended and her gaze locked with his.

"Wife?"

"I rather botched that, didn't I?" Aston gave her a boyish, lopsided grin. "I cannot promise you a life of luxury and extravagance, Chasity. But I can offer you one of comfort and happiness along with my enduring adoration and devotion."

He fished around in his coat pocket and pulled out a small royal blue velvet box. Opening the lid, he exposed a stunning oval sapphire and diamond engagement ring.

"Oh, Aston." She blinked rapidly against the moisture misting her eyes. "It's simply stunning."

He lifted her chin with his forefinger, his brown eyes so full of love that tears filled hers. "Marry me, Chasity. I am only complete when I am with you. I cannot conceive another day, let alone a lifetime, without you. I love you beyond words, beyond everything."

"Yes. Oh, yes." She held her hand out, and Aston slipped the ring on. "Yes, I will marry you."

"It's a trifle large, but I'll have it sized, my darling." He took her mouth in a reverent kiss, and Chasity had no doubt this man was her soul mate.

She still grasped the other letter, and it crackled when he tightened his embrace.

Glancing down, Aston saw the rectangle and shook his head. "You've not read your other letter. Why don't you read it while I see to Roi, and then we can go to dinner?"

"Perfect." She turned it over and scrunched her forehead. "It's from Mrs. Shepherd. She's the proprietress at the foundling home where I was raised." Settling onto a chair near a lamp, she used her thumbnail to break the wax seal.

Aston had just opened the door when she cried out.

"Chasity?" He rushed back to her and knelt before her. "Darling, what is it?"

Chasity couldn't get the words past her tongue. She shook her head and thrust the letter at him.

Aston rapidly read the short letter. Sitting back on his heels, he whistled as he passed it back to her unsteady hand. "Your father is alive, and your grandfather was a duke?"

All sorts of emotions churned in her stomach: joy, fear, uncertainty, leeriness, excitement, anticipation, and wariness.

"I never considered that my parents wanted me. I've always assumed I was an unwelcome by-blow. Something to be ashamed of. To learn my parents were married, and my father didn't know about me..." She sucked in a ragged breath. "And this man..." she skimmed the letter again. "This Martin Oxley-Norton wants to meet me."

"Do *you* want to meet him?" Aston gently asked.

Chasity slowly nodded.

"I think I do. He has suffered too these many years." She grasped Aston's hand, needing his unwavering strength. "But only if you go with me, Aston. I don't think I'm brave enough to meet him alone."

"You are the bravest woman I know, and I am positive you would do fine on your own. But I'd like to meet my future father-in-law."

Aston scooted onto the settee and drew her into his arms.

She nestled into his side and rested her head on his chest, one hand wrapped around his trim waist. He smelled like soap and starch and Aston.

"You write to him and pick a day and time," Aston said into her hair. "Just not tomorrow afternoon. Uncle Conley's funeral is at four."

Tilting her head back, Chasity cupped his face with her palm.

"This has been the most extraordinary day. I'm to marry the love of my life, the keeper of my heart. What's more, my father is alive and wants to meet me. I'm practically giddy with excitement and anticipation." She gave a rueful shake of her head. "And to think yesterday I believed my world had been turned upside down, and I had no future."

"Now your future is with me, my love," Aston murmured into her hair.

Stretching, she kissed him. "God has blessed me so."

"And me as well." He caressed her cheek, then rested his chin atop her head. "Chasity, I'd rather not wait until my period of mourning for Uncle Conley is over for us to marry. I want to make you my wife as soon as possible if you have no objections."

No objections whatsoever.

"I want that too. Let's have a small, private ceremony with only our closest friends present in a fortnight."

"Perfect, darling." Aston kissed the crown of her head. "How does a honeymoon in Italy sound?"

"Absolutely divine," Chasity whispered as she drew his head down to hers, and all thoughts of their dinner plans faded away, replaced by anticipation of a future with the man she loved.

EPILOGUE

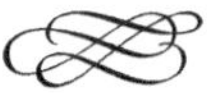

Mrs. Shepherd always said that God can work all things for good, but I tell you, Chasity, Theran Rutland is the exception. There isn't a reverent bone in the man's body. And I must endure his impossible company for three and a half more weeks! This house party is testing every ounce of my Christian charity and patience. I'm delighted to hear of your marriage. I so wanted to attend the wedding, but the Ceddes wouldn't permit me the days off to travel to London. I wish you and your Mr. Terramier a joyous future.

~ Miss Purity Mayfield in a hastily
scribbled letter to Mrs. Chasity Terramier
while her charges played Blind Man's Bluff
Sent but lost in the post

London
Berkeley Square
Sutton House
17 January 1819

Aston wrapped an arm about Chasity's slender waist and kissed the sensitive spot just under her ear as they climbed the stairs. She wore another of her new gowns, this one a lovely long-sleeved, sky-blue morning gown that flattered her creamy skin and indigo eyes.

He glanced up, taking in the stately home's architecture. Sutton House didn't feel as oppressive or dark without Grandfather's tyrannical presence. Or perhaps it was Chasity who'd brought light and happiness into the house. She sang or hummed as she went about a myriad of tasks, and a smile almost always graced her lovely features.

"Aston, it's the middle of the afternoon," Chasity admonished in a scandalized whisper as he hurried her along the corridor. However, she didn't resist. "Whatever will the servants think?"

They passed Josie and another maid carrying soiled linens, and the pair burst into muffled giggles.

Chasity had little trouble convincing Josie to come to work for her and Aston. The impudent minx winked at Aston and tossed him a grin over her shoulder.

He grinned back.

"They'll think I love my wife very much indeed."

More than Aston had ever thought humanly possible in truth. And that love grew every single day. No man deserved this much happiness, and not a day passed that he didn't thank God for blessing him by bringing Chasity into his life.

Chasity groaned and pressed her cheek into his arm. "Or that I'm a wanton, and you're a libertine."

"Not a bit of it." He gave her a playful wink. "I pay them too well to think any such thing. I've no doubt they are far happier and more content with me as their employer than they ever were working for my grandfather. And I know Josie is delighted to be in our employ."

Everyone was happier.

Aston most of all.

Chasity had met her father, and they were forging a cautious, yet warm relationship. The Rt. Hon. Martin Oxley-Norton had never remarried and was eager to become better acquainted with his only child.

That she was the granddaughter of a duke would've sent Aston's snobbish grandfather over the moon with delight. *If* he'd been made aware.

He had not.

Before Aston had married Chasity, he'd explained Werner's terminal illness.

"Chasity, you will one day become Lady Woolbury. I know that was not something either of us foresaw, but you should be aware of exactly what you are agreeing to."

Aston hadn't expected her to cry off, but nevertheless, he couldn't in good conscience marry her without telling her Werner was dying and that she'd be a viscountess one day soon.

"Names and titles mean naught to me, Aston. Being your wife is all I aspire to and all I need to keep me content until I'm gray-haired and wrinkled. When you inherit, we'll deal with the title's responsibilities together."

In point of fact, Aston had essentially taken on those duties when he'd banished the viscount to the Borderlands. Everyone from Viscount Woolbury's solicitor to the scullery maids had expressed their approval of the new arrangements. Aston had also paid Werner's legitimate debts.

Werner had asked Aston and Chasity to move into Sutton House once they were wed, but Aston wouldn't consider it unless Chasity agreed wholeheartedly. She had, of course. There wasn't a selfish bone in her body.

"He's your cousin, Aston. Naturally, we shall go to stay

with him and help in any way we can to make his life more comfortable and peaceful."

She'd also eagerly agreed that Mrs. Longsdon should become their cook. After Aston had helped his former landlady hire a married couple to run her boarding house, Pearl Longsdon happily moved into Sutton House. The food she'd served at her lodging house had been delicious, but with an unlimited budget and several maids to assist her in the kitchens now, each meal was a culinary masterpiece.

Aston had postponed their honeymoon to Italy, and his co-investors had supported his decision to stay in London until Werner passed. Chasity too had insisted they should wait.

"Werner is the last of your kin, Aston. Take this time with him. We have the rest of our lives to go to Italy."

Bedridden now, his health increasingly failing, Werner had become quite close to Aston and Chasity. She read to him—he was particularly fond of the Psalms and Cowper's poems, and Aston played the violin for his cousin.

When the physician Aston had hired had called last week, he'd taken Aston aside. "Mr. Terramier's heart has weakened to the state that he may very well pass in his sleep at any time now. There's nothing to be done but to keep him comfortable. I shall visit again next week. Send for me if his condition worsens."

Aston hadn't told Werner his prognosis, though he suspected his cousin knew his end was near. He would miss Werner, and it saddened him that his cousin would never know the happiness Aston had found.

Aston reached the bedchamber he and Chasity shared and pushed the latch down.

Chasity glanced furtively up and down the passageway

before slipping inside the opening. "You are utterly scandalous, husband."

"But you love me regardless." He gave her his most rakish smile.

"And well you know it," she said on a pretend pout.

Aston followed her inside, then soundlessly closed the well-oiled door. The key made a slight scraping sound when he turned it in the lock. "I simply want to give my lady a lesson in love."

Chasity came to him and, standing on her toes, pulled his head toward hers. "The teacher has become the pupil."

He grinned as he lifted her into his arms. "A most apt pupil, indeed."

If you'd like to leave a review, I would be grateful.

Keep reading for a free preview of
HIS ONE AND ONLY LADY
Secrets of Scandalous Ladies, Book Four

HIS ONE AND ONLY LADY
Secrets of Scandalous Ladies
Book 4

That man is an ogre! What an impossible predicament you find yourself in, Faith. I know how much you anticipated your new position as an amanuensis for Lord Kellinggrave. He only retained you because he lost a wager, you say? I do believe his lordship is a despicable knave for misleading you. For what it is worth, I applaud your intrepidness and gumption. Do not let the scapegrace chase you away. I know you, Faith, and you shall make an excellent scrivener. His lordship shall learn as much if he puts aside his masculine prejudices. I hope to visit you and Chasity, Joy, Mercy, and Faith soon. My tenure with the Ceddes family is ending as Pomeroy is off to Harrow and the girls to boarding school this autumn—the poor dears. After eight years, I've grown very fond of the children and shall miss them dreadfully. But alas, time ticks relentlessly onward, and I must search for a new position even while I'm at the Mumfords' house party. I shall pray I never have an employer as impossible as your Lord Kellinggrave.

~Miss Purity Mayfield, in a letter written en route to the Mumfords' to Miss Faith Roth

Mottford Hall, Essex, England
Home of the Earl and Countess of Mumford
22 August 1818 — Mid-Morning

Bliss. Pure, sublime bliss.

Purity Mayfield tilted her face into the sun's soothing rays and gave a contented sigh. Humming the ballad she'd sung to her wards that morning, she relaxed into the comfortable, cushioned chaise lounge—one of several in the cozy garden. Apparently, none of the other houseguests who'd arrived over the past couple of days had discovered this magical retreat yet.

To be honest, she wasn't exactly one of the elite *haut ton* guests. Nevertheless, she felt as privileged as one at that moment. Glancing around the isolated enclosure, Purity smiled.

Her cherished privacy might be partially due to the ten-foot-tall beech hedge surrounding the charming square and its distance from the manor house. She'd accidentally come upon the hedgerow's arched opening while walking the greens farthest from the opulent mansion.

A few feet from her, across the verdant grass paralleled by rust-colored brick pavers lay a square pond. An angel wearing a strategically placed loincloth for modesty's sake topped a two-tiered burbling fountain.

For the moment, this enchanted haven was all hers to enjoy. No quieting energetic children, wiping noses, gently but firmly reminding her charges to mind their manners, or doing the often unreasonable bidding of her employers.

For a few coveted minutes, it was just Purity, the fish, a few bees, and a mild August morning sun.

She eyed the entrance with a mixture of trepidation and expectation.

Surely this heaven was too perfect to last.

The reluctance of the upper ten thousand to part with their plush mattresses before noon also likely explained why no others had joined her in this picturesque retreat.

That was perfectly fine with Purity.

More than fine, in truth.

In general, the upper class had little use for servants except how the menials made their elite lives more comfortable and convenient. Respect, consideration, and basic politeness were reserved for those of the same social standing as members of *le beau monde*—not the lower orders.

As a governess, Purity fell somewhere between the servants and the family she worked for. She wasn't included in either, and it made for a rather lonely existence—apart from her time with the children in her charge.

As accomplished as she was at appearing subservient and compliant, there were moments she had to bite the inside of her cheek to keep her ungracious opinions to herself or stifle a disrespectful, if honest, retort.

Her current employers, the Viscount and Viscountess Ceddes, were challenging on the best day and intolerable on a bad one. She'd long since learned to recite in her head, "a soft answer turneth away wrath," over and over.

Never mind how much *she* might fume after a disagreeable encounter. Her position, and thus her future, depended on an acquiescent and submissive demeanor.

Neither trait came naturally to her.

She'd often wondered if either of her parents—she had no idea who they might be—had possessed a tenacious nature too. Or which she'd inherited her riot of curly hair from.

Shading her eyes with her hand, Purity spied a squirrel cautiously creeping across the grass. Sitting on its haunches, it darted its black-eyed gaze here and there, its tiny little nose twitching all the while. The darling thing would advance a couple of feet, flick its fluffy red tail, and repeat its anxious perusal.

Perhaps it drank from the fountain daily.

Purity lowered her hand, and the squirrel dashed into the hedge. A second later, it poked its head out and scolded her for her audacity.

She chuckled. "I'll be gone soon, my little friend. Let me enjoy these few stolen moments in paradise before my world returns to normal."

Drumming her fingertips on the chaise's arms, Purity permitted her mind to return to her earlier reflections. To be fair, disagreeable interactions with Lord and Lady Ceddes had been infrequent since they seldom deemed it necessary to visit their offspring.

Attending this house party was an unofficial send-off for Pomeroy, Merrilee, and Amaris Bardslay. It was also the longest expanse of time the couple had spent with their children since they'd hired Purity. Neither parent demonstrated paternal inclinations. Ten minutes with their offspring stretched the bounds of their benevolence.

In just over four short weeks, Purity's charges would be off to boarding schools, and she would be unemployed for the first time since leaving Haven House and Academy for the Enrichment of Young Women—the foundling home and school where she'd been raised and educated.

Hopefully, she'd manage a visit with a few of her closest

friends, also raised at Haven House and Academy for the Enrichment of Young Women, before she started her new job.

A job she'd yet to acquire, as she had no letter of reference yet.

She'd waited for months—growing increasingly impatient—for her employers to offer to write her a recommendation or even mention that, very shortly, her services would no longer be required. They'd remained frustratingly obtuse and disobliging in that regard. Now, she found herself in the discomfiting position of having to ask for a reference while in attendance at this house party.

She made a dismissive sound in her throat.

Enough of this unfruitful, melancholy musing.

With deliberate intent, Purity turned her thoughts in a more pleasant direction: this glorious, unforeseen reprieve from responsibilities. She'd been given an unexpected gift, and she meant to enjoy every splendid second.

After breakfast, Lady Ceddes had actually collected her children for a morning outing with several other families and didn't require Purity's services for a few hours.

Would wonders never cease?

There *was* a first time for everything.

Purity gave a slight shake of her head, and a curl flopped loose from her chignon.

Dratted nuisance.

An unremarkable light brown, her hair had vexed her since girlhood when she'd been required to wrestle the unruly mass into a neat knot by Hester Shepherd, the headmistress at Haven House and Academy for the Enrichment of Young Women.

Once Purity had captured the strand fluttering about her face in the fragrant honeysuckle and rose-scented breeze, she confined the wayward curl with a pin. Giving her hair a satisfied pat to ensure no more intrepid tresses were about to spring loose, she settled into the luxurious chaise lounge once more.

She determined nothing would stir her from her current contentment.

When was the last time she'd had an entire morning to herself?

At Petherwick Court, the Ceddes primary estate in Somerset, a myriad of tasks always needed attending to if the children were engaged elsewhere. Governesses of three energetic children seldom were permitted such a luxury. Governesses to self-centered aristocrats such as her employers, who seldom saw their offspring, even less so.

And yet here she was. Unfettered by her three charges and without a single duty to perform. In all of her eight years employed by the Ceddes, this was a first. A most pleasant and welcome first, indeed.

Crossing her ankles, Purity grinned, feeling very much a pampered lady of leisure.

The sensation was both disconcerting and delightful.

She wiggled her toes in her practical black half boots and furrowed her brow at the frayed hem of her slate blue gown. Now wasn't the time to add to her scant wardrobe. Best to wait until she found a new position and then acquire an appropriate new gown or two.

Drowsy from the sun's warmth, the comforting buzz of engorged gold and ebony bees zipping from fat blossom to even fatter blossom, and the sweet warbles of songbirds, she permitted her eyelids to drift shut.

Awaking with a start, she snapped her gaping mouth closed and touched a fingertip to the side of her mouth to catch the unladylike dribble of drool perched there. Goodness, she'd been far more tired than she'd realized. Thank the Lord there hadn't been anyone about to see her lack of decorum.

Furrowing her brow, she glanced around.

What had awakened her?

She'd heard something. Something—no, *someone*—in distress.

Head cocked, she listened keenly past the sounds of the frothing fountain, humming bees, and chirping birds.

There.

A faint sniffle and a muffled sob.

Rising, Purity perused the square enclosure.

Nothing.

Another pitiful sob cut through the garden's tranquility.

The thread of sound came from near the entrance.

Did someone hide in one of the nooks created by the zealously tended beeches on either side of the tapered arc? Purity had been so entranced with this oasis that she'd scarcely paid the weathered stone benches nestled there any mind when she'd stumbled upon the secret garden.

Swiftly making her way across the expanse, her shoes and skirts swishing against the short grass as she went, she approached the opening. As she neared the entrance, Purity slowed her pace when she spied a little girl's tousled red hair.

At the dejected little form huddled there, Purity's heart wrenched, and she pressed a hand to her bosom.

Dear Lord. The poor darling.

I hope you enjoyed this free preview of
HIS ONE AND ONLY LADY
Secrets of Scandalous Ladies
Book Four

FROM THE DESK OF COLLETTE CAMERON®

Thank you for reading LOVE LESSONS FOR A LADY. While this is a sweet Regency with inspirational overtones, I also attempted to tastefully introduce romantic elements and sexual tension.

In my books, I strive for historical accuracy. Women of quality had few reputable employment choices open to them during the Regency era. If a woman lost her position, she faced prostitution and starvation. It can be challenging for modern readers to grasp how much the peerage disdained those amongst their ranks who actually earned a living. The very nature of aristocracy was that they did not work, which quite often meant their coffers weren't nearly as full as they pretended. Aston's grandfather's objection to his grandson "smelling of the shop" was a firmly held ideal amongst *le beau monde*. Even speaking about money, or the lack thereof, was considered vulgar.

I gave you a few hints regarding the next books in the series. The fourth book in my Secrets of Scandalous Ladies series is HIS ONE AND ONLY LADY. As you might have already guessed, Purity Mayfield and Theran Rutland's tale is an enemies to lovers romance. Book five in the series, Faith Roth and Constantine Kellinggrave's romance is NEVER A PROPER LADY. Expect a few sparks to fly between them too.

I mention some of Aston's closest friends and co-investors in his marble quarry. These are their stories if you are interested in reading them:

Bradford Kingsley (Viscount Kingsley): A ROGUE'S SCANDALOUS WISH, The Honorable Rogues® series

Manchester Sterling (Marquis of Sterling): A ROSE FOR A ROGUE, The Honorable Rogues® series

Ian Hamilton (Viscount Warrick): THE VISCOUNT'S VOW, Castle Brides series

Ewan McTavish (Viscount Sethwick): HIGHLANDER'S HOPE, Castle Brides series

Bartholomew Yancy (Earl of Ramsbury): VIRTUE AND VALOR, Highland Heather Romancing a Scot series.

I have another important point I'd like to briefly touch on. Recently, a reader outside the United States became upset that I used American spellings in my Secrets of Scandalous Ladies series, which is set in Regency England. I use American spelling in all of my Regency and Highlander series.

Multiple factors go into an author deciding which spellings to use for their books. I chose American spelling simply because most of my reading audience is American, and my books are published in America. While I stick to a few British rules, such as I shall and I shan't instead of I will and won't, I haven't extensively adopted other British grammatical rules and spelling. I believe my readers are flexible enough to adapt to slightly different spellings. After all, it's the romance novel that matters, right?

To stay abreast of the releases of the other books in the Secrets of Scandalous Ladies series, you can subscribe to my newsletter or visit my author world at collettecameron-books.com.

I hope you enjoyed a romantic escape for a few hours with Aston and Chasity. If you liked their story, please consider leaving a review.

Hugs,

Collette

If you haven't joined Collette's exclusive mailing list click on QR image to sign up! You'll get access to exclusive content, sneak peeks, contests, giveaways, and more...

(P.S. No spam!)

https://collettecameronbooks.com/freegift

**Collette loves to hear from readers.
You can contact her via her website: collettecameronbooks.com.
Or email her directly at collette@collettecameronbooks.com.**

**You can also follow Collette on social media:
Facebook:** https://www.-
facebook.com/ColletteCameronNovels/
Instagram: https://instagram.com/collettecameronauthor/
Goodreads: https://www.goodreads.com/collettecameron
Book Bub: https://www.bookbub.com/authors/collette-cameron

Pinterest: http://www.pinterest.com/colletteauthor/
YouTube: https://www.youtube.com/@ColletteCamero-
nAuthor

Giggles are Guaranteed
Collette's Cheris Reader Group

If you love to chat about all things romance-book related and enjoy taking part in fun and engaging live events, contests, and giveaways join **Collette's Chèris VIP Reader Group, https://www.facebook.com/groups/CollettesCheris/,** my exclusive private book group on Facebook.

Giggles are guaranteed!

Hope to see you there,
Collette Cameron®

COLLETTE CAMERON®

USA Today Bestselling author Collette Cameron® is renowned for her captivating, humorous, and heartwarming Scottish and Regency historical romance novels. With over 65 published titles, over 1.6 million books sold around the world, and multiple writing awards to her credit, Collette is a well-known author in the world of historical romance.

Readers love her witty and relatable characters including daring rogues, dashing scoundrels, and the strong and spirited heroines who capture their hearts. From the rugged highlands to the refined drawing rooms of Regency England, Collette's novels will transport you to another time and place, where love and adventure are just a page away.

Collette's Sweet-to-Spicy Timeless Romances® are the perfect escape for readers looking for romantic escape, poignant inspiration, engaging humor, and entertaining stories.

Based in the Pacific Northwest, Collette is surrounded by the lush greenery and rainy skies that inspire her writing. She dreams of one day splitting her time between the Pacific Northwest and Scotland. In the meantime, she indulges in her love of all things cobalt blue, dachshunds, chocolate, and of course, crafting her next historical romance.

Blue Rose Romance® LLC
collette@collettecameronbooks.com
collettecameronbooks.com

The Wallflower's Wild Wager — Book 1

The Spinster's Secret Stake, Book 2

DUKES COME CALLING

A Sensual Marriage of Convenience

Regency Historical Romance

A Diamond for a Duke — Book 1

Only a Duke Would Dare — Book 2

A December with a Duke — Book 3

What Would a Duke Do? — Book 4

Wooed by a Wicked Duke — Book 5

Duchess of His Heart — Book 6

Never Dance with a Duke — Book 7

Wedding Her Christmas Duke — Book 8

The Debutante and the Duke — Book 9

Loved by a Dangerous Duke — Book 10

How to Win a Duke's Heart — Book 11

When a Duke Desires a Lass — Book 12

My Dearest Duke — Book 13

FOR THE LOVE OF AN EARL (Wicked Earls' Club)

A Humorous Aristocrat and Wallflower

Regency Romance Adventure

Earl of Wainthorpe — Book 1

Earl of Scarborough — Book 2

Earl of Keyworth — Book 3

Earl of Renshaw — Book 4

HEART OF A SCOT

A Passionate Enemies to Lovers

Scottish Highlander Historical Mystery

Romance Adventure

To Love a Highland Laird — Book 1

To Redeem a Highland Rogue — Book 2

To Seduce a Highland Scoundrel — Book 3

To Woo a Highland Warrior — Book 4

To Enchant a Highland Earl — Book 5

To Defy a Highland Duke — Book 6

To Marry a Highland Marauder — Book 7

To Bargain with a Highland Buccaneer — Book 8

A Christmas Kiss for the Highlander — Book 9

HIGHLAND HEATHER ROMANCING A SCOT: CASTLE BRIDES

A Passionate Enemies to Lovers Second Chance Scottish Highlander Mystery Romance

Heart of a Highlander — Prequel

The Viscount's Vow — Book 1

The Highlander's Heiress — Book 2

The Earl's Enticement — Book 3

Triumph and Treasure — Book 4

Virtue and Valor — Book 5

Heartbreak and Honor — Book

Scandal's Splendor — Book 7

Passion and Plunder — Book 8

Wishes and Wonder — Book 9

A Yuletide Highlander — Book 10

SECRETS OF SCANDALOUS LADIES

A Romantic Class Difference Forced Proximity Regency Romance with Aristocrats

A Lady's Scandalous Kiss — Book 1

No Lady for the Lord — Book 2

Love Lessons for a Lady — Book 3

His One and Only Lady — Book 4

Never a Proper Lady — Book 5

Lady Tempts a Rogue — Book 6

THE CULPEPPER MISSES
A Humorous Wallflower Family Saga
Regency Romantic Comedy

The Earl and the Spinster — Book 1

The Marquis and the Vixen — Book 2

The Lord and the Wallflower — Book 3

The Buccaneer and the Bluestocking — Book 4

The Lieutenant and the Lady — Book 5

THE HONORABLE ROGUES®
A Second Chance Redeemable Rogue
and Wallflower Regency Romance

A Kiss for a Rogue — Book 1

A Bride for a Rogue — Book 2